PRAISE FOR BOLDER DREAMS

Reminiscent of *Once a Runner*, the great 1978 cult classic that inspired a generation of competitive runners, *Bolder Dreams* beautifully captures the gawky geekiness of the passionate high school runner searching for excellence and adolescent self-awareness. Bobby Reyes nails the unique camaraderie that exists within a cross country team, vividly depicting its power to create lifelong memories like no other sport. Amusing, thoughtful and poignant, *Bolder Dreams* will be deeply evocative for anyone who loves competitive running. I couldn't wait to find out if Baxter won the race of his life, and I was rooting for him.

John Meyers, *Denver Post*

I've been familiar with Bobby's work for years. He is passionate about running. The sport comes alive in his writing because he has lived it. *Bolder Dreams* serves as an inspiration to anyone who competes at a high level or runs to stay in shape. Bobby's stories – they are not all about running – are unique and work well in pulling the reader into his unique and crazy world. This is a one-of-a-kind book and definitely should be added to every runner's home library.

Danny Summers, *Colorado Springs Gazette*

Few books about running capture high school athletics and life inside the hallways so perfectly, and Mr. Reyes's fictional portrayal of one runner's quest for that elusive win does just that. *Bolder Dreams* is an engrossing novel that keeps you hooked from start to finish. It's the kind of book you don't want to put away at first read.

Cory Mull, MileSplit USA senior editor

BOLDER DREAMS

A CHASE FOR SUCCESS AND ACCEPTANCE

BOBBY REYES

Bobby Rey (signature)

ILLUMIFY MEDIA GLOBAL
Littleton, Colorado

The views and opinions expressed in this book are those of the author
and do not necessarily reflect the official policy or position of Illumify
Media Global.

Published by
Illumify Media Global
www.IllumifyMedia.com
"Write. Publish. Market. *SELL!*"

Library of Congress Control Number: 2020915431

Paperback ISBN: 978-1-947360-66-2
eBook ISBN: 978-1-947360-67-9

Cover design by Debbie Lewis

Printed in the United States of America

CONTENTS

Part III:

About the Author

PART I

1

MORNING SHAKEOUT

The morning joggers were out as usual.

Those florescent tights and shirts and hats and socks glimmering underneath the Colorado sun. Runners in Hokas, Boosts, *Five Fingers*.

In Boulder everyone works out in the morning.

Running the iconic trails barefoot. Riding on $8,000 Trek bikes. Hiking the Flatirons in Oboz and an "authentic" walking stick from REI purchased for $90. Hundred-dollar yoga classes with chia seeds and fro-yo.

Whatever it is, in Boulder, you do it in the morning so you have something to brag about the rest of the day. Winner gets to gloat until tomorrow morning, when everyone gets up to do it all over again.

The South Boulder Creek trail had that usual hum that accompanies a highway—only with runners. Groups of twos and threes jogged on lightly, and then there's that occasional pack of a dozen or more from one of the many post-collegiate Boulder training groups that use that

3

coveted "Boulder" tag in their group name like it's unique.

Oh, we're so clever.

We'll do the time-honored low-key wave or gentle nod as we cross paths.

Occasionally I'll pass a beefy Crossfitter with headphones and tattoos or a buff mother with veins streaking down her arms pushing a baby stroller.

We're all passing cars on the highway to nirvana, or something like that.

Boulder.

Yeah, it's a little different from everywhere else. It's its own unique bubble of Red Bull-pumping fitness freaks and soul-searchers. If you don't work out, you don't exist.

And me?

I was one of them.

I was a runner, to classify myself in the particulars.

Some kids played football or soccer or tennis. I ran. It's what I did, and in high school circles, I did it well.

Well, well enough.

Well enough to see my name in the state rankings, which, let's face it, once you've made it there, you're practically signing autographs after cross country races or at track meets. Finding your photo featured on MileSplit or on their Instagram page is like placing your hands in that cement on the Hollywood Walk of Fame.

I didn't have my Hollywood star on the sidewalk just yet, but I was getting there, one mile at a time.

And speaking of one mile at a time, the August sun was just peeking over the trees to the east as I cruised along the path at a pace I wasn't keeping track of. *Leave your watch at home.* Behind me the Flatirons loomed tall over the landscape. Those jagged rocks spit up from the earth and can be seen from over thirty miles away on clear days. They're like *Big Brother* or the *Running God,* always watching, always monitoring effort, always keeping time.

And in that moment, I felt that slicing judgment of my own effort, because I was stumbling through my morning run as easily as possible—just leaning forward and letting gravity pull me along.

My eyes were still waking up from another sleepless night, but my body seemed to already be moving along like on an automated conveyer belt. Sometimes I didn't even have to think on those early morning runs. Just get up, and let the body do its thing.

A summer's worth of ten- to twelve-mile days will do that to you.

Perhaps the light crunch of dirt beneath my feet was a bit of an early morning meditation. There's that rhythmic cadence: right foot, left foot, right foot, left foot, right foot, left foot. I could sleep through the whole process, but on that morning my mind was already up and way ahead of my body.

It was the first day of my last year of high school, and while every other kid my age was likely gelling their hair to cemented perfection, I was out there getting in some mileage with the rest of Boulder's community of distance addicts.

I'm not much of a morning person, but when I am, it's only to run. Beyond that, leave me the hell alone. I can't function much before 9 a.m., but if I'm running, then we're all good.

It's the simplicity of it that makes it doable for me,

like the White Stripes—the simplicity that made them famous works across all genres of life.

The sound of the creek is soothing, and I was trying not to fall back asleep. I saw a pack of runners a decade or so older than me cruising along shirtless at a five-minute clip of effort and silence, and I marveled at how they were still doing this running thing. For a moment I wondered if that would be me one day, still having a go at this, or maybe I would hang it up by then.

Who knew?

We passed like strangers, strangers doing the same thing, and for a moment I got lost in the huffing and puffing of a true effort. It was a symphony to my ears, one that I'd grown accustomed to growing up in the bubble. When they passed, a breeze followed them, and once they were around that soft corner heading back west toward the Flatirons, the air went silent again, and I could hear the water rushing down the South Boulder Creek to my right.

My mind warped to the creek crossing before that hill at Penrose Stadium. The blur of noise, those screaming mothers and fathers and friends and teammates and coaches. The intensity in the air: *a State champ will be named today*. I could feel the warmth of someone beside me, their arms swinging up the hill between the barns— that hill the sun beamed down on without hesitation, the hill with the loose dirt and little rocks. My arms swinging up the hill.

I could see golden tips on the leaves of the trees to my right, and right beneath them more screaming people. It's an overload of senses, and it's the final 600 meters of the State championships, and *everyone* is watching.

I slapped my fresh face back to reality, back to this quiet morning five-mile run. I couldn't go to State just yet; I had to be here, here in this morning run before school. Here along the creek, passing Maggie's Tree and those colorful flowers of love and nostalgia.

Here. In. This. Moment.

I tried to stay there. I took a deep breath and smelled a lilac tree. I didn't see those light purple tips when I passed, but I smelled it, somewhere. There wasn't a cloud in the sky, and that deep blue canvas spread over me.

I thought of what was ahead—the first day of my senior year. Art class. History. English. The afternoon workout of 4xMile with a three-minute recovery; that dreaded third mile where you're just trying to get through because you know you'll find something on the last mile, but you can't let the pace lag here.

Flash.

The second hill after passing the creek, the one leading to Penrose Stadium. That familiar burn in the legs and the lungs. When it all connected near the end of a race and everything seemed red like a balloon that's about to explode. But I felt it then, the disconnect between me and whoever is breathing down my back. One step. Two steps. Three steps. And I could feel the rubber band between us finally loosening. Then, there it was: the break.

I was gone. Moving up and away from whoever was chasing me. Freddy Krueger or some mass murderer, the past, my depression, *whatever*.

It was behind me now.

I was free, and nothing was holding me back.

I could still feel it, the chase, but I could feel the

momentum too, that downhill spiral, but I was going up, up to where I got to leave it all behind me and become something *more*.

A State champion.

An added bold line to my running resume.

I was between the crowd behind me at the hill and the crowd inside Penrose Stadium. I was hovering between two moments in time: before and after. All I heard was the crunch of loose dirt beneath my spikes and my breathing. All there was was hope, hope that this moment would not last forever, because this was *painful*, and hope that no one would ruin it.

Then, there it was.

I turned the corner, taking a sharp right around the edge of the stadium, and the crowd came to life. I saw them, all those colors in a mixed bowl, and they saw me, alone on the course without a shadow. They roared to life, and so did I. Into the stadium I went. Destiny awaited, and I was speeding toward it.

I didn't hear anything in particular, just that roar, and it was music to my ears, or a bag of purple Skittles and cream soda on a Saturday night: dessert.

I poured on the pace, pumping hard, and it didn't seem so difficult anymore, because I could see the bright red paint across the dirt and that huge white sign over it in bold capital letters: FINISH.

The light at the end of the tunnel—*is this what death feels like?*

There was no one between me and this absolutely beautiful sight in the front me, like the first time I saw the Pacific.

I knew it was mine now. I knew the State title was

mine. The title I'd wanted for so long but could only dream of. The title I won sooo many times in sooo many ways on those dusty trails all summer long.

And now, this moment right here, the dream becomes a reality. I threw my hands up in victory like I did so many times in my head on morning runs.

And then I realized.

I realized.

I was still on one of those morning runs, and State was three months away.

Dammit.

2

FLATIRONS HIGH

FLATIRONS HIGH IS ONE OF THOSE SCHOOLS THAT has a long list of stars. A few years ago a rap duo called The Bangarang Boys dropped their first album, and it quickly went platinum. When it did, they paid homage to FHS by shooting their first music video from their hit single "Get Your Crouton" in the halls with the bright red lockers. Since then the phrase has become synonymous with winning State.

There have also been a few astronauts, an MLB short-stop, a Denver Bronco, and a Pulitzer Prize-winning author.

So as you can see, it was pretty difficult to stand out in a school with such a laundry list of superstars.

Add all that to the fact that FHS was ranked the top public school in the country for a few years. After that article rich WASP moms and dads moved to Boulder simply to have their kid walking these hallowed halls. When that happened, the value skyrocketed, and all of a sudden FHS was a cool-kid place to go to school.

All that money coming in meant that the school lunches went from iceberg lettuce to romaine and spinach mixes, the football field went from shady beige grass to turf, the basketball court was remodeled with a newly designed Falcon at mid-court, and best of all, the track was resurfaced with mondo material.

You get where I'm going with this.

Walking down the hall in pleated khakis or Wranglers was *no bueno*. And for me, it was all I had.

Clad in some old Adidas Marathon 10s and the latest cross country meet shirt, it was my style, and I don't mean that in the positive sense. My "style" came with a sort of girl-repellant. Perhaps it was the pleats, or the old running shoes that still held my dried sweat from last summer's run up El Dorado Canyon.

I don't know.

Or perhaps I do—I'll go ahead and own this. My style, or lack thereof, wasn't doing me any favors. I'd have to win races before that would come.

Subaru. Lexus. Mercedes.

No, I'm not talking about the outside of a business park, I'm talking about the parking lot outside FHS. Kids with their parents' money, or parents gifting their used cars to kids with newly minted licenses so they wouldn't feel guilty buying a new one for themselves.

Boulder.

I didn't have either. I just walked to school because my parents believed if you live within a mile, you walk.

It was additional training, better for legs anyway to loosen up after the morning shakeout.

If Kenyans run six miles one way to school, I could walk one. Besides, I had a State title to win in ten weeks

The parking lot was buzzing, as if everyone was excited to be back at school. I never shared their enthusiasm—school was never really my thing, but it did mean the cross country season was just weeks away, and that fact did send a ripple of blood pumping through my veins.

I walked between the rows of shiny cars with the curls of my hair dangling over my ears, still wet from the post-morning run shower.

I thought of the song "Icky Thump" by the White Stripes and that raw guitar solo. I walked a little slower and pretended there was a camera hovering just over my left shoulder as I made way through the double doors for the first time of the year one final time.

I was the hero in my own music video, here to conquer, yeah, I'm not sure.

"Hey, Baxter!" Coach Andrews said, speed-walking out of the double doors, ruining my slow-motion entrance. He had his traditional teacher outfit of pleated khakis and a short-sleeve flannel tucked in. "How was the shakeout this morning? Easy like we talked about, right?"

"A little sore," I said. "Still feeling Saturday's long run in my legs."

"Comes with the territory," he said with laugh.

I could sense we were two passing trains. He had somewhere to be.

"Remember, we've got those mile repeats later," he said, turning his gaze back toward the parking lot. "Big year!"

"Can't wait!" I chirped.

"All right, I've got to get to my car and back before the bell. I'll see you this afternoon."

"See ya, Coach!"

Back to that thump. Thump. Thump. Ra-ah-rah!
Thump. Thump. Thump.

I'm not sure why I'm being all dramatic with this
entrance thing. Life is just cooler with a soundtrack.

My first class of the day was physics, and I'll be
honest, it's a subject that is very clearly not my forte. That,
along with it being 7:45 in the morning, my brain hadn't
quite woken up yet. I needed at least two miles of light
jogging and some strides before I'd be ready to step on the
start line for a race of any distance. My brain worked the
same way when it came to my education.

Give me till, say, 9:00 a.m.?

While I was no physics buff, one good thing about
the class was that I had Coach Bradford. He was the boys'
basketball coach and was clearly a basketball guy himself
—his large six-foot seven-inch frame took up the doorway
when he entered his classroom, which was a rectangle of
stone countertops with sinks and gadgets I couldn't
explain. He was the kind of coach-teacher combo that
wore the pleated khakis with a navy blue Polo embroi-
dered with "Falcon Basketball" nearly every day of the
week. He never went a week without a trim and shaved
every morning before the half-hour commute to school.

He spoke with a deep, hallowed tone and chuckled at
his own jokes. I'd have titled him a Forever Bro if he
hadn't been married with kids, but he still had the sense of
humor to mingle with us kids half his age. If he hadn't
been teaching a subject I wasn't really interested in, I'd
probably have liked him more.

I took a seat in the back right corner, which is the seat
I coveted in nearly every class. It was the closest to the

door and the farthest from the front of the class. I could blend in between all the colors back here, and doodle or discreetly read, or space out.

If there was anything I learned on that first day in his class, it's that when you smell a fart, technically you're digesting it.

Coach Bradford sniffed the air and made a face when he shared this before booming with laughter and slapping a basketball player on the back. "Now you know," he said, chuckling at this tidbit of useful information.

Around our cross country circles we referred to farts as "beef," as in: "You like my beef?" before wafting the scent of our ass in each other's faces. Usually the contents of what you were smelling followed: "That's two Slim Jims, a donut, and a cappuccino."

Smelling each other's beef would never be the same.

Coach Bradford's class came and went with a few jokes, and some fear of this whole we're-taking-a-quiz-every-Friday thing. I was horrible at tests and quizzes, and basically any sort of subject that required sitting in one place for a long time. My legs jittered with the anxious-ness of a coming run or workout or race. My mind bounced off the cement walls that resembled a prison.

I got a little relief, mentally speaking, in second period, which was Art II. Miss Shonda wasn't exactly a fun teacher like Coach Bradford, but last year in Art I she let me play my Incubus album while we painted.

And speaking of painting, I loved to paint. I was in no way good at it, but it's just soothing. Like meditation.

The previous year Miss Shonda gave me an 80% on our final end-of-the-year art projects, which I titled "Where's The Light Source?" after her comment on my piece two weeks earlier. She said it with a smug grin, her hands out. I was pissed in the moment but played it off by honoring her with the title.

Beyond that moment, art with Miss Shonda wasn't too bad. And it supplied me with an unlimited amount of paint.

The swaying of the brush on a smooth canvas, and the paint—oh, the paint. I'd come to enjoy watercolors. The blending of the two colors to create one, and then if you messed up you could still push the paint around the canvas to create something different entirely. There was something about creating something new that I found appealing; it was like a race: every course was different, the weather, the competition, the way it all played out. No two races were alike.

One of my favorite classes was English, and that's for multiple reasons.

Most of the class time included writing essays and reading. Two of my favorite things. That, and of course there was Mrs. Blake.

Oh, Mrs. Blake. . .

The object of nearly every teenage boy's affection.

Mrs. Blake was a petite woman in her late twenties. Unlike most of the teachers who wore floral prints and blow-dried hair, Mrs. Blake found her way somewhere between being an adult and a kid. She wore long, striped skirts that hovered just above her ankles and form-fitting blouses with fluffs on her shoulders.

She wore her hair short and lightened on the tops with dark roots. I found this part strange, because I typically didn't find the short-hair thing appealing, but on her it totally worked. Perhaps it was because it exposed her tan neck and flawless skin. Those big brown eyes stare into you and she could get anyone to mindlessly agree, "Yes, Mrs. Blake. . ." in hypnotized tones.

Oh, yeah, and she was the cheerleading coach, but she didn't wear it. She was almost too cool for it, because she had an assertiveness that seemed like she didn't like taking orders—she gave them.

She was one of those insanely well-read English teachers who could cite anyone at any given time, so naturally when she spoke, we all listened.

Additionally, Mrs. Blake was the one teacher who seemed interested in cross country—because she read the newspaper sports pages.

"The team looks like they're going to have a good year, don't they?" she asked when I took my seat in her class, those big brown eyes beaming in interest.

I melted into my seat.

"Yes, Mrs. Blake."

Her soft touch on my shoulder was the golden prize. All other boys pouted in jealousy that she not only acknowledged my presence, but touched my bony shoulder.

Yes, Mrs. Blake. . .

The first day went off without a hitch, and I was relieved, because we had mile repeats on the training docket for the afternoon. So I ate a light lunch with anticipation, or anxiousness of what was on the menu for the afternoon: pain.

We met for practice in the wrestling room since there wasn't exactly a spot for the cross country team.

Two years before we'd started an impromptu Fight Club, which quickly ended after Austin Clevenger broke

Tony Shumberg's collarbone. We had a solid ten minutes to create an alibi before Coach Andrews came. We all agreed that Tony falling backward on his backpack seemed plausible.

Skinny kids play-fighting never really was a good idea.

One by one the team trickled in, gabbing about the day, freshmen looking relieved to have survived their first day of high school, sophomores smug in their new place as not-freshmen, juniors relieved to be halfway through high school, and seniors, all-important seniors, ready to lead with perhaps too much pride, I'll admit.

The scent of IcyHot, sweat, and body odor lingered in the air while our numbers climbed just over thirty bony bodies while we waited for Coach to arrive.

Coach Andrews, better known more simply as Coach, was my favorite person.

Two years earlier he was my only friend when I first moved to Boulder and didn't know anyone on the team. Of course this quickly made me the least-cool kid on the team. It also didn't help that I barely made the varsity squad. But that all changed when the miles started to show up in my legs, and I finished fourth at State my junior year. Then I wasn't so much of a nerd. Well, technically I wasn't a nerd. Being fast and a cross country runner makes you cool—on the team, that is. In the halls and among the rest of the school, it was a gray area. In some circles you still didn't exist.

Coach showed up with his clipboard in hand, sporting a freshly shaven black goatee, and in his traditional post-school day attire: long navy blue running shorts, the ones without the cut, light gray t-shirt with

"Flatirons XC" in gold across the front, and a navy blue hat.

He was tall and lean—the look of a distance runner.

Two years at the helm of the cross country program and he already transformed a team that had never made it to State to finishing third last year.

I liked to think our ascension was systematic.

"All right, guys." He slapped his clipboard to get our attention, which was never easy, to get few dozen high school boys to settle on one thing, unless it was a girl.

"I hope everyone had a good first day," he continued.

I stood near the back like a seasoned vet. I had done this first-day-of-school thing with Coach three times now.

"Just a reminder, if you haven't already, you need to get me your physicals or you can't race this weekend, okay?"

Nods across the room, then of course there was always that one freshman who missed the memo, even if Coach had been saying it the past two weeks during our summer practices. A hand raised. New kid. Didn't know him.

"Coach Andrews," he asked with a shaky voice. "When do I have to get it to you?"

Coach bypassed the moment to be a jerk and kept his cool—he taught freshmen English, so he was used to this sort of dumb question. He looked at his clipboard then back at the shaky freshman with glasses with sweat marks.

"Connor, right?" he asked, more like a statement.

The kid nodded.

"Connor, like I mentioned, you have to get it to me by Friday, or you can't come to the stage races, okay?"

The kid nodded.

"Did everyone hear that?" Coach asked louder now.

"You have to get me your physicals by Friday, or you *cannot* come to the stage races."

Nods were plentiful.

"Any more questions?"

I pled inside my head for no more questions. I was ready to get this shindig rolling. We had mile repeats on tap for the first time that season, and I was curious as to where I was compared to last year.

We'd done this workout the first Monday of school the past two years—this would be the third—and so far I'd gone from averaging 5:49s my sophomore year to 5:28s junior year.

Coach kept a book of our workouts so we knew where we were last year at this time, I also kept one for myself.

"No more questions?"

This time it was a real question.

Please no, please no, please no. . .

"All right, let's get going! You guys know the drill. A warmup mile for everyone except Baxter, Blake, Todd, John, and Josh. Two for you guys."

Our top five ran most of the summer together. I say most, because Chester had a girlfriend. So he typically committed to run with us in the morning then backed out if she stayed the night. He was a real stage-five clinger sort of guy, so when he had a girlfriend he only existed at practice, and that's because he had to be there.

We headed out to circle the lake twice. It's where we'd be working out.

The paved loop around the lake was almost exactly one mile. Coach measured it out years ago and found it about thirty meters long, so we had a separated starting and stopping point for each interval.

The sun beamed bright overhead. In Colorado, it might read only seventy-five or eighty degrees, but it always feels hotter because of the proximity to the sun— we're closer because of the elevation, so the sun is always a bit more intense.

And what added to the intensity was that the one mile path around the lake offered very little shade.

The pack shuffled behind us five.

Blake was already talking about some new girl in his history class, perhaps one he followed into school hours earlier.

"She's totally hot," he went on. "Get this, she was wearing those jeans without the back pockets. They were practically see-through. Bright pink, man. I give it one week, and I'll have at least my arm around her."

Blake was the classic soccer-player-turned-runner and more of the ladies' man among our squad. He didn't run track the previous year because he played soccer, but we were really working on him to commit to running fully. He had a big, unconventional frame for a distance guy, but last year as a sophomore he broke seventeen without training in the summer—just summer soccer league fitness. His strides were big and powerful, and they appeared to come with a ton of effort, but he had a big engine. When he reached top speed it was like he was born to run. He was smooth and fast, and insanely competitive.

You could say Blake was my best friend, or one of my better friends. I wasn't sure if I was one of those people who had a best friend or just one of those people who didn't. It had never really been a focus. But I could sort of consider Blake a best friend since we shared most of the miles on the trails all summer long, then would go hang out at his pool while baking under the sun.

"Oh, please," Todd said. "That's only if she doesn't meet me."

We called Todd One-Step Todd because he was that guy who always had to run a step in front of us, no matter what the pace. This almost never worked during races or work-outs, but on warm-ups and our daily runs he was always one-stepping. This almost always prompted either me or Blake to mess with him by ramping up the pace so he would run himself into the ground trying to remain one step ahead of us. He was sort of an oddball with a false sense of confi-dence—he *wanted* to be a ladies' man, but the reality was he didn't have game like Blake. He was tall and thin like me, so he had that distance-runner look. He swayed back and forth with his long arms when he ran, but he was light on his toes and faster than Blake last year. But Blake did a lot of work over the past summer, and he was clearly stronger.

Chester ran on in silence, somewhere in his own mind, probably thinking about some sexual escapade with his current girlfriend.

The previous week he'd skipped practice because he was "sick." So we ran over to his house to check in on him and caught him and his girlfriend doing the no-pants dance on his couch. Never look through the window of an unsuspecting teammate who claims to be sick but is really banging his girlfriend. You'll come to regret it. Trust me.

The image of his tiny body and thin legs poking out underneath his girlfriend is something I wished I could wash from my head with bleach.

Curiosity killed the cat.

Chester was actually more talented than Blake and Todd, but he knew it, and that's what held him back from being better. So he did half the work over the summer— well, let me rephrase: half the *running* work. I'm sure he worked out. . . with his girlfriend.

This obviously made Blake work even harder. Chester had a small frame, like former 5000 American record holder Dathan Ritzenhein, and an insanely efficient stride. He was the only guy on the team that could usually hang with me over the longer tempo runs.

On the other side of the spectrum, John, who we all referred to as "the fro" for his insanely curly afro, was one of the hardest workers on the team but had perhaps the least amount of talent. He made up for it, however, by outworking nearly everyone. He'd been a junior varsity guy last year but went mile-for-mile with Blake over the summer.

Sweat dripped down my elbows and the sides of my face, and I thought how we hadn't even started the workout yet. I didn't miss these hot summer workouts much, but soon it would be cool and the leaves on the trees would be changing. Then it would really be cross country season.

After nearly fifteen minutes of running around the lake with Blake gabbing about hot history girl and Todd challenging to steal her, we looped back to the team and went through our normal routine: plyos, stretching, and chugging water before heading to the makeshift line on the pavement.

"Already everybody knows the workout, right?" Coach

said. "Three-by mile for everyone except Baxter, Blake, Todd, John, and Josh, then a three-minute rest."

We strolled over to the starting line, shaking out our limbs.

I was always nervous in these moments, even just the workouts. They were like practice races where you didn't know how it was going to go, but you hoped.

And there was always that tiny slither of fear that it might not go well, or that it would hurt a lot. I'd come to grips with this fear thing. I told myself: *this is going to hurt like hell, and if it doesn't, you're not running hard enough.*

Anticipating the pain had worked so far.

Coach stood by the line with his clipboard in one hand, stopwatch in the other, and two more dangling from his neck.

"All right, guys, remember: pace yourself. It's not about the speed. It's about doing all of what's on your sheet. Run the pace that will get you through the workout. If you go too fast the first one, you still have to run two more—remember that, okay?"

Nods across the board, but there was always at least one over-eager sophomore or junior or freshman who would go out too fast, die, then have to jog their way home. I knew this because that was once me.

"All right, everybody ready?" Coach lifted his stopwatch in the air like a starter's gun.

Here. We. Go.

"Go!"

Off the line we went.

The path curved to the left within twenty meters, so I took off a little quick to get the jump on the rest of the team. I wanted to run the tangents and not an inch more.

Todd did his usual one-step which would last maybe a quarter mile, while Blake hovered a few steps back, and Chester ran on my heels.

We took the curve and cruised by the fire station on the right. There was a little dip where the path crossed the road, and every time we approached the station I hoped those sirens wouldn't go blaring—we were already into the interval. No turning back.

Around the station the path headed downward for the next quarter mile. I leaned forward and took this free energy. I tried to relax my arms as they swung forward and listened to the heavy breathing around me.

When we passed the first 400—the thin aspen tree with no leaves on the right—I checked my watch.

1:16.

Little fast. . .

Behind me I could hear the shuffle of the team starting to spread out. The second quarter was where I tried to relax a little more because it was about to get a lot harder. I took a glance at the lake to my right and saw the Flatirons reflecting off the motionless water.

The water looked appealing. I'd have loved to just ditch this interval and go dive in and call off.

But there was work to be done.

Down the gradual hill we went, and Todd was already struggling. Somewhere behind me Blake was looking to eat him up and spit him out, and Chester was biding his time—he preferred to sweep people up in the end.

Sandbagging, as I called it.

There was a sharp downhill to the wooden bridge that signified the halfway point, and it was followed immediately by a steep uphill that we called the Wall for its steep but short feature. It was steep enough to cut your stride, but short enough to leap up, about twenty meters, then the hill got gradual as we climbed through the trees. This was the only shaded area of the path, and it's where I made the first of my two or three moves during this workout.

I liked to practice surging early, because then I could avoid having to kick, a skill I lacked.

At the halfway point we were at 2:39, and there were still four of us.

Up the Wall I pumped my arms a little more to create a gap and then the surge. It was the gradual hill that separated us. Now I got to work.

We climbed through the trees and Todd was now falling off, Blake ready to sweep him up, and Chester hovering behind them all.

The hill topped out with 600 meters to go, and it flattened for maybe 100 meters before we climbed another fifty-meter hill that looked out over the makeshift soccer field. I poured on the pace like I imagined all summer long. This was how I would rid myself of company on the cross country courses this fall—a long, drawn-out surge to the finish.

I could feel the dry, high-altitude air burning in my lungs as I came out of the trees and back to the exposed path. That lake water still looked good, but now I could almost see the finish.

Blake, Todd, and Chester were working out their placings behind me, and I was off, free to run up front without a challenger.

I climbed the final hill and felt the burn pulsating through my lungs, legs, and arms. This was how it would be this weekend. Feel the burn. Embrace the burn. Love the burn.

Search for more.

Now the watch was inconsequential. This wasn't about time, it was about effort. I reminded myself to lift my knees, pump my arms, lean forward, don't let the bear jump on your back.

Over the crest of the final hill there was a solid 100 meters between me and catching my breath for three minutes. I saw Coach standing tall but tiny all the way down the stretch beside the fence, stopwatch in hand.

"Let's go, Baxter! All the way through! All the way!"

I could hear his shouting down the path, and I pumped all the more. I wasn't just running for me, I was running for him. I was his star pupil, his guinea pig, his project. My success meant his success.

The heat was really getting to me now, but I tried to shake it off like the sweat dripping from the backs of my hands.

"5:12. . .5:13. . .5:13. . ."

Coach read off the clock as I neared the finish. Not. There. Yet.

I leaned, leaned, leaned forward to catch the end of the clock.

"5:16!" he yelled out, clicking the top of his stopwatch in a gotcha as I crossed the makeshift finish line.

I slowed to a jog then a walk while the burn in my lungs settled to a more manageable effort.

He continued to read out the clock as Blake came sprinting in with Chester on his heels, and Todd a second back.

"5:21. . .5:22. . .5:23. . ."

They staggered in, huffing and puffing. I made my way toward the water cooler in the little figure-eight walk I did between the trees each interval. That allowed me to keep time without looking at my watch. Three figure eights equaled three minutes.

"Good start, good start," Coach said. "Three minutes, and we're back on the line."

He turned back to the straightaway, clock in hand, as the rest of the team came in.

Oh, cross country had started.

3

THAT MAGICAL EVENING HOUR

HOME WAS ON THE TOP OF A SLEEPY NEIGHBORHOOD with views of Table Mesa. It was on the southern-most tip of Boulder, and in many ways, its own version of the bubble because we could see just outside of it.

Denver always sat in a haze of smog from all the cars, and on a clear day you could see the tip of Pikes Peak an hour and a half to the south.

It was that magical evening hour where every mom or dad starts cooking the night's meal, and you can smell it sifting out of open windows. Working parents would be coming home to the scent of steaks on the grill, potatoes in the oven, or spaghetti on the burner.

Outside of morning runs down the creek, the scents of the evening had to be my favorite. My mom was always cooking something that pleased the nose and the stomach. That orange glow of the kitchen light lit her tan skin while her green eyes scanned the contents of the bubbling water on the stove.

Our home was something out of a catalogue, or it felt

that way. It was one of those places that you were afraid to touch things, because you didn't want to break them.

The tables were all shiny mahogany, stained to perfection by my dad at some point. The couches were long and cushy, and rarely used. There were untouched plates with unique designs, proof that they were handmade by the peoples of some other country. Rugs were the centerpiece of every room, and most of them were darker hues. Paintings and intricate drawings lined the walls, visuals of my father's time in the military. There were drawings of buildings at West Point, paintings of his time in Argentina, and photos of his many accolades.

Most rooms were ones to walk through rather than to sit in.

The only room of the house, besides my own, that seemed to get a lot of use was the kitchen, which is where we spent most of our time.

A long beige table sat along the long wall with three placemats, and plates and glass cups and silverware sat in their spots. Like everything else in this home, everything had its spot, its home.

Dinner was a fairly tame affair, though it was the one time of the day that we'd all sit and regroup from the day, namely, it was when my father would ask what I had accomplished.

Every day had a purpose, and every day required that you fulfill that purpose.

In my own dictionary of meanings, this meant that the day's purpose was to rock those mile repeats.

And sometimes that meant napping to ease the soreness from the morning run, but Dad never really counted napping as something that had purpose.

Through his eyes, things that had purpose typically required physical effort or made money. Like tossing a Frisbee across an open field and chasing it in an attempt to catch it before it fell. Or seeing how many push-ups you could do before your arms gave out and you face-planted into the carpet. Or working twelve-hour days, seven day a week overseas in combat-heavy places like Baghdad for some multi-billion dollar company supplying American forces with miniature cities to call home, like he did ten months out of the year.

The kind of stuff that made six figures at the minimum—if you made money, it didn't matter exactly what you did, because you made money.

That was Dad.

A retired military vet who called life among civilians "bullshit."

When the Iraq war raged and American troops landed in the desert, it was my dad who was in charge of logistics for one of those many corporations you may recognize on TV but I can't name here. "Contractors," they're called.

And they were paid to make sure American money was well taken care of.

I'm not sure where or when I took a hard-left off my dad's train—okay, maybe I do—but somewhere along the way we took separate paths in terms of our moral or philosophical obligations to this world.

It's why we typically avoided clashing on controversial topics at the dinner table—he had his way about life, and I had mine, and somewhere in the middle was my mom, who always had a way of keeping the peace.

Perhaps it was her homemade spaghetti, which she taught me how to make since Dad was gone most of the year, and she was working. In my version of the meal I always tossed out the onions. Never could stand them.

Dad was all about the end result, whereas Mom was definitely more about the journey, which is something we shared, even though I don't think she ever picked up on that fact—that we had more in common than, say, her and my sister, Myra.

See, my mom lost her mother when she was nineteen years old. They were best friends all the way up until the end, which wasn't exactly a surprise—her mother had a heart condition that took her at forty-three years old.

Ever since that day when they parted ways, my mother yearned to have a daughter of her own, a new best friend.

And she got that with Myra, sort of, who not-so-ironically enough had my father's ability to command a room.

Myra lived an enormous amount of distance away from home—a solid sixty minutes without traffic to Fort Collins. And I say "enormous amount of distance" as a bit of a joke. The distance was monumental when she first moved out for college since she couldn't rush home for dinner ever night. She was out pursuing a degree in whatever my dad deemed worthy of his affections. Destined to be an FBI agent or something with a laminated badge and a big paycheck.

Mom drove up I-25 every weekend Myra didn't drive down, which didn't happen often. Myra needed laundry done, and my mother gladly washed, dried, and folded it for her in a fresh white laundry basket for her to take back to her fourth-story dorm room that looked just like home. Matching bed sheets and pillows with matching bins to fit precisely beneath the bed where her folded clothes would sit. Hung-up shirts in color-coordinated rows in her closet. Leather boots and running shoes lined neatly beneath them. Hand-created coffee mugs, made in Ouray, part of a "going-away" gift from me.

There wasn't anything in her room that didn't look straight out of a catalogue.

For my mother's efforts Myra would confide in her about her relationships, and she'd give her a hug on the way out, and a "See you next week."

My mother didn't mind—it was getting the affection of her sought-out daughter.

And somewhere in between all of that I fit. More so as the black sheep. Every family needs that oddly shaped puzzle piece to fit somewhere. I guess that was my role, and I'm not quite sure when I learned to embrace it, but somewhere along the way I realized I had to, for the sake of survival.

They never really understood the intensity I put into running or my odd sense of humor, for that matter. Anything of mine they couldn't grasp was "a Baxter thing," explained only under the context of: "I never really understood where you came from."

Adoption was never really a suitable explanation, because my sister and I were junior version of our parents with various mixtures of physical similarities. I had my dad's height and facial features with my mom's Puerto Rican tan and curly hair.

I never questioned that they were my actual parents, but they clearly saw some oddities within me.

My dad accepted these differences once I started winning races and splashing across the sports pages—that might not be money, but it was status, which, in his eyes was like money.

Mom would cut out the newspaper articles, like she did for Myra, and place them neatly on the fridge, which was about the only place in the house where you could find my face.

I had more play in other people's houses than my own.

Perhaps it's why I chose to stake out my claim on the courses *outside* my home.

That was the beauty with running—the strongest survived. There was no way to talk your way to the finish line before anyone else.

It was perhaps the only objective thing in my life, which is why I clung to it.

And for perhaps the second time in my life, my ambitions seemed to line up with my father's. Ever since the preseason rankings dropped and my name found its way into the Top ten State rankings, it all of a sudden gave him a reason to chat me up about my own pursuits. They mattered now.

"How was the workout, *mijo*?" He typically referred to me as "mijo" or "son" in his more fatherly moments, like at the dinner table while filling his plate with mashed potatoes or slicing his steak. Once the meal began, however, he wouldn't converse until he was done, which never took him long.

"Good. Mile repeats. Faster than last year, so I'm ahead." I eyed him cautiously. Improvement was a good thing, but it had to be *enough*. It was just enough to improve. I needed to be better-than, or more specifically, The Best.

"It doesn't matter what you do in life as long as you're the best," he once told a younger version of me. Bowl haircut and all. I made all-county chorus that year.

"Good, mijo." He nodded in approval.

This effectively ended the conversation as my mother brought dishes with steak and mashed potatoes to the table. When the food arrived my father always went silent —the purpose shifted from catching up to eating, and he never multi-tasks. Now the purpose of the moment was to eat.

After a few moments of clanging steak knives and forks, my father let out a satisfied exhale. It normally took him about three minutes to eat, maybe less, because he never engaged in conversation. Meanwhile my mother and I took our time—I'd lather each slice of medium-well steak with copious amounts of A1 sauce. I liked to enjoy each bite of whatever it was I was eating.

"So, mijo," he brought the conversation back to life. "Are you ready for the race this weekend?"

"Totally," I said between bites.

"Don't talk and eat," he shot back. "Finish what's in your mouth, then speak."

Yes, sir.

"I think today's workout shows I'm at least twenty seconds faster than this time last year," I explained. "Over two miles, so yeah, I'm feeling ready."

"Yes, not yeah."

"Yes."

"And I believe Myra said she might come down this weekend," my mother jumped into the conversation. "I'm not sure if she'll go to the race, but she said she's thinking of coming down Friday night."

She beamed with the excitement of the possibility of an entire weekend with her daughter. Dad too.

"Well, make sure she stays in Saturday night. I'd love to catch up," he said. "She's always coming and going."

"You know your daughter," my mother quipped. "Just like her father."

There was a detectable ting on that last quip, but my father seemed not to notice, or perhaps chose not to care.

4
_____

THE STAGE RACES

HARLOW PLATTS PARK WAS BUZZING IN EXCITEMENT. Reds, blues, greens, yellows, purples. Color everywhere. Long yellow buses lined along the neighborhood streets, cars backing up into spaces, the scent of Bengay lingering in the air, freshly cut green grass, packs of runners left and right, sweat, singlets with bold lettering, "Boulder," "Highlands Ranch," "Valor," "Longmont." Moms with cameras. Dads in baseball caps and sunglasses.

On top of it all, the Flatirons loomed above in their godly stance, watching over every performance across the land below. Those beige rocks splitting upwards toward the heavens and all the green trees hiding in the shadows between them.

Down below, the zoo of the stage races was well underway. White chalk lines lined the course from the slanted hill, over to the lake, along the sidewalk, stopping just before the wooden bridge, then restarting on the other side, hugging the lake, then back to the big hill that leads up to the school, around the big tree to the left, then the low gradual downhill back toward the start.

Teams camped out alongside the course by the sidewalk on the hill in all their crazy colors.

The first meet of the year always came with a little extra anxiety. It's the first true test of your summer fitness.

Based on our workouts, I knew I was in better shape than last year, but there's always that evil, doubtful question: *are you?*

I barely got a wink of sleep the night before.

We jogged along the sidewalk on the other side of the school by the track. I hated warming up on the course where everyone else was. I wanted to get into my own space, my own head, without all the circus on the other side of the hill.

The stage races were a unique, one-of-a-kind of race. There were five races or stages, starting with the slowest and moving upwards to the fastest. Stage 5 would have your fifth runner race against everyone else's fifth runner, stage four would have your fourth runner, stage three has your third runner—you get the idea.

The setup prompted every team to pit their best runner against each other in one race, and so on.

While Coach had really dismissed the importance of this race, I still ran with a little extra nervousness streaking through my blood.

"Remember, it's the end of the season that matters, not the beginning," he said last night at our spaghetti dinner. The basil-flavored homemade spaghetti still sat in my stomach, but damn it was *good*.

This would be the first test, not only of fitness, but of where the state stood. After finishing fourth last year, I was the top returner, but rankings don't mean anything, and I knew that much. I knew I'd have to prove it.

And in my way would be Grant Hemingway, the junior from Valor.

A year ago he was the only sophomore to make it to the State track meet in the 3200. I watched from the sidelines as he bulled his way around the track in a 9:36—four seconds faster than my PR.

He was a chesty runner with a powerful stride and a stoic presence, like the Russian from *Rocky IV.* The word was that he ran ninety-mile weeks over the summer and did 1,000 push-ups and sit-ups a day.

I can barely do ten pull-ups.

The only time we had raced each other was last year at the State cross country meet, but he was a different runner then.

This would be our one and only meeting this season, excluding the State meet, so I knew this would be the one time I could get a read on him and figure out his weaknesses.

Every fifteen minutes the starter's gun shot off, sending slithers of smoke into the air and a jolt of anxiousness through my veins.

I laced up my white Nike Zoom Victory spikes. The scent of sweat still lingered on the shoestrings. I hadn't spiked up since last track season, when I finished third in the 3200 at Regionals, missing State by two seconds.

Two seconds.

They had regional t-shirts being made with "See You At State!" on the back. When I passed them with my mother she offered to buy me one, not seeing what it said on the back.

I lamented, "Sure, and I'll add 'NOT!' in black marker."

She missed the joke.

I vowed then that I wouldn't be out-kicked in another race. Missing the State track meet by two seconds was more than enough fuel to rage through my body all summer long, but Grant Hemingway and his ninety-mile weeks was enough to make me cower down like a puppy still learning where and when to piss.

I only hit eighty-two once and over eighty three times.

Would that be enough?

When you come out of the woods of summer training you can't go back and add miles. You just have to hope you did everything you could, and that it would be enough.

Dammit, Grant Hemingway.

The gun shot off again, sending stage 2 off into the ether, and I knew I'd be next. This meant I had about fifteen minutes to get to the starting line, do some strides, and let it rip.

After sliding on my spikes I felt 100 pounds lighter, like my legs could do anything, or almost anything. I jogged over to the starting line where Coach was standing, clipboard in hand, navy blue Polo with "Flatirons" in gold across the right chest, matching navy blue hat, pleated khaki shorts, and a pair of Nike Pegasus. We had our uniforms, he had his.

"So, you remember the plan?" said. He pursed his lips, deep brown eyes digging into me. I could see the worry in him. This was a nerve-wracking experience for him too. We were his product. Was it good enough? Did he set us up with all the right tools?

There'd be a season to accurately answer that question, but this would be the first test.

"Yes," I said, shaking out my arms in nervousness. "Get out strong, front pack through the mile, around five minutes, then surge, see who goes, if anyone comes, wait, then surge again with 600 to go."

Coach nodded along in agreement, hand hiding his mouth, eyes cast down like he was seeing the race unfold as I repeated what we discussed the night before.

"Good," he said. "And remember, it's just the first race, so feel it out. If you feel good, go, if not, it's okay."

He let the last word trail a bit. There shouldn't be any reason not to feel good, minus the five-mile tempo we did three days before where I averaged a career best of 5:42, but it was still only August, and there was a ton of races ahead of us.

He patted me on the back as he passed to head toward the finish where Chester was sprinting in in fourth. He had a good day—if he had a good day, so could I. Right?

I set my sights back on the open field in front of me, the Flatirons looming high to the west. Here we go. The first race of my last cross country season.

I stood tall in my box and sprinted out to feel the grass beneath me. My quads were still a little sore, but everything else felt intact. I pranced off my toes over the thick green grass and tried to find my stride, the one that could carry me along the course. Nearly twenty feet to my right Grant Hemingway was doing the same thing. He squinted under the Colorado sun and looked like he could run through a wall.

I tried to forget him, and forget everything I thought

I knew. *Be here. The past doesn't matter, all that matters is this.*

The starter blew his whistle, meaning we'd have another minute before being sent off to battle. I jogged back to the starting line, taking my place among the masses. I tried to yawn to settle my lungs. I read somewhere that yawning before a race was good thing, so I made a point to try to yawn, ease my breathing, and prepare for the painfest ahead of me.

The starter lifted his gun high into the air for the fifth time of the day, and nearly 50 of us leaned forward along the white chalk line, ready to start the race and our season.

"Racers to your marks! Set. . ."

The gun!

We hurtled into the field like wild beasts, and I felt claustrophobic in the moment. I pumped my arms to make space and bound off my toes, down the gradual hill before a short twenty-meter jump up to the flat part of the course.

The crowd stood on top of this mini hill and cheered as we roared by. When we cruised by the quarter-mile mark the pack thinned out a little and I took a peek to my right, searching for Grant Hemingway.

Grant Hemingway.

He was just five feet to my right, alongside an unknown runner, probably some sophomore who had a good summer and was a little over eager.

I took my spot on the left side of the lead and let Mr. Unknown take the pace, which felt honest. I was relieved we weren't blasting away at a sub-4:45 mile, because then we'd really be in some pain later.

We headed south along the path between the trees with the lake to our left and the Flatirons to our right. Around the bridge and back toward the circus, the pack dwindled down to four with Grant Hemingway still mimicking me on the other side of Mr. Unknown. I kept a steady eye on him because I knew it'd come down to either of us in the end. We climbed up the hill and around the big tree on the left, dropping a few more bodies behind us.

When we circled back to the starting line, which was right next to the finish line, I heard Coach through the masses: "Right there! Right there! Steady, Baxter! Steady."

He cupped his hands around his mouth and clapped as I ran by. I could hear the nervousness in his voice.

"4:49. . . 4:50. . . 4:51. . ."

The numerals read off in bright red at the mile marker. That's about where I was hoping we'd be.

Here we go. Surge number one in three. . . two. . . one.

Ignition.

I leaned forward and threw in a quick surge, Tour de France-style. I spent July glued to the race and decided to adopt the road-cyclist style of attack: fast and furious, and brief.

More just shaking out the legs and seeing who has gears, and who doesn't.

I jumped up on my toes and attacked hard for about 200 meters, enough to rid myself of any shadows.

And for a moment it almost seemed like it worked.

Back down the hill I couldn't feel Grant Hemingway on my shoulder following my little ambitious burst, but he climbed back.

Grant Hemingway .

Back out between the trees he let me control the pace, but I could see him casually running out of the corner of my eye. This dude was a machine.

Well, that's it for Plan A.

I regrouped, feeling the burn in my lungs now, and had to hope that the next move would be the final kill shot.

But he ran ninety miles a week. All summer long.

Doubt flooded my head as the fear of his superiority leaked through my dam of confidence.

One thousand push-ups and sit-ups a day.

We ran in tandem across the wooden bridge, spikes sticking a little too much. I listened to the hollow echo, curious if we had any chasers, or if it was just down to us.

Just us two.

Well, that's good to know. If I die a little, I can still hold on to second.

The first loser.

Back along the flat grass path to the finish, and one more time up the steep hill to the big tree we went, stuck together with the invisible rubber band.

For a moment confidence came flooding back as I realized he hadn't once surged on me, he hadn't once tried to run away from me.

Maybe I can beat him.

I perked up as we neared the 600-to-go mark, a tiny little pinecone I placed next to the course so I knew how much was left, and I punched the air.

Rocky vs. Drago.

Here we go.

And there it was again, a little bit of distance, not comfortable enough, but a little. That's all I'd need.

Down the gradual hill it was all in front of me now. I could see the throngs of people on both sides, leading inwards to the finish line an upside down V. The colorful flags lining the way.

I kicked hard once more down the hill, less than 300 meters now, and then I felt it. I felt *him*.

Grant Hemingway responded. *Hard.*

He kicked by me like I was standing still. A child racing a man.

Apollo vs. Drago.

Dammit.

I watched him power off and away, helpless to do anything. I tried to dig further into my well, but I was clear out of water.

The crowd cheered, but I couldn't do anything. We neared the finish line, and I watched him raise his arms ever so slightly in victory.

Grant Hemingway 1, me 0.

5

DISCOUNTS AND DESPAIR

"WE'LL DO THE MEAL, WITH PEPPERONI, HAND-tossed, salads, and breadsticks instead of soda," I ordered for the group.

Abo's Pizza was dimly lit, with the traditional red-and-white checkered table cloths with the parmesan cheese sitting in the middle. Usually by the end of our visit the top would be loose and cheese would be spread all over someone's pizza as a prank. I was usually the first to do it —I'd take the parmesan cheese and spread some on my pizza while loosening the lid with my pinky and thumb simultaneously, this way everyone else thought it was still tight.

Oh, high school shenanigans.

Abo's Pizza had this deal that if you got the meal, which was two large pizzas, a trip to the salad bar, and soda, it was only $20, but if you substituted sodas for the waters, you could get breadsticks too. More food is always better when you're at the table with a handful of hungry cross country runners just hours post-meet.

Going to Abo's the night after a meet became a thing about a year ago, when Blake and I were driving around aimlessly in my white Corsica listening to the new Incubus album when he had a pizza craving. I'm always up for pizza, so we went to Abo's and bam. It became a thing.

The group expanded quickly, including John and a few girls from the cross country team, usually Lily, and Sherry, and sometimes Monika.

We sat at the long booth in the corner by the fake candlelight. Outside the dark windows the sun had already set, and our stomachs were empty.

"I'm telling you, Grant Hemingway is legit," Blake went on. His man-crush was already making me envious. *Or is it jealousy?*

"Totally," John agreed. "The kid is a man. Did you hear about all the push-ups and sit-ups? That's crazy. Baxter, how many can you do?"

"Nowhere near that," I lamented, trying to hide my fear and jealousy of the new star of the course.

Grant Hemingway.

"And he has, like, biceps," Blake went on. "And did you see his abs? You can wash your clothes on them. He's totally cut."

"You sound ready to jump his bones," Lily chimed in with a sly smile before sipping on her straw. "I'm not sure if I should be freaked out that you're staring at a guy's body, or what."

I was glad somebody said it, because I didn't want to talk about Grant Hemingway. I was already thinking about that sprint and how I couldn't hang.

If I can't beat Grant Hemingway, I can't win State.

"Oh, shut up, Lily. Don't hide the fact that you're thinking what I'm saying," Blake shot back.

Lily's big brown eyes went wide as she giggled nervously with Sherry.

"I'm just saying," she said. "It's a little weird that you're talking about some guy's body."

She sipped on her straw again with those tight lips.

Lily was cute, but I couldn't tell if I liked her yet. Or if she liked me.

As if I had a choice.

She had this light tan, soft skin and brown hair that gently curled as it went down to her shoulders, but it was those big brown eyes that caught me. Seductive is the best word, even though I doubt she knew it. She had only dated one guy, and they barely even kissed—she claimed he was a horrible kisser, so I knew seduction wasn't exactly her thing. *Or maybe it was.*

She was witty, smart, and she always had some flowery scent radiating off her.

Perhaps it wasn't that I didn't know if I liked her, it was that I was intimidated by her. She could make anyone look like an ass—not that making Blake look like an ass is hard, but she had some quick response to every sentence out of someone else's mouth.

"And I'm just sayin'," Blake continued on. "He made Baxter look like he was standing still, and he just ran 9:31 in his first race of the season."

"Ouch, man. . ." I chimed in, unable to avoid it anymore.

"I know, dude," John said, shaking his head. "Baxter is sitting right here, right here, and you're confessing your love for Grant Hemingway."

He gestured to my chair as if I wasn't sitting in it as Blake tried to backtrack out of the hole he had just dug himself.

"I didn't mean that, like, Baxter *can't* take him." He stumbled through his words, trying to find his thoughts. "I was just saying, you know, that, like, you gotta give it to him. He just ran a 9:31 on grass and dirt, and like, won, and you know, beat Baxter."

Ouch.

I clutched my chest like I had just been shot and laughed to hide the fact that losing actually did hurt, but I couldn't let them all see that I was worried more than they were talking.

"Dude, Blake, we gotta be on Baxter's team—we literally are. We want Baxter to get *his* crouton, remember? Not Grant Hemingway." John half-hugged me and patted me on the back. "He's our dude, *dude*."

"That's one dude too many," Lily said with a laugh. Those big brown eyes glimmering underneath the pale yellow light that hung above our table. Our eyes locked for a brief, hesitant moment, before I quickly diverted my attention to the bright white lights over the salad bar.

I'm *that* awkward guy.

"All you guys talk about is Grant Hemingway this, Grant Hemingway that," she went on, shaking her head toward Sherry, inviting her in on the conversation.

Sherry was the quiet best friend. She had long, straight red hair and light blue eyes. She wasn't nearly as assertive as Lily, but she brought a light humor to the group. She was almost always smiling or laughing. She made anyone feel like they were funny, even if they weren't.

"I'd think Blake was in love if he didn't talk about other girls so much," Sherry said.

"Or maybe he goes both ways," Lily joked.

"Oh, please," Blake jumped in with a chuckle. "I'm not into dudes, you guys all know that, you particularly, John—remember that night I told you about what I had with Sarah? Yeah. I'm just saying he's fast. That's all."

Lily rolled her eyes at Sherry as they shared a sly smile. *Oh, to be in their heads in this moment.*

"And on that note. . . I'm getting a salad." I slid my way out of the booth while Blake continued on with his confession of love for Grant Hemingway.

After grabbing one of those clean white plates that are stacked high I turned to see Lily right behind me. I felt a heat wave surge through my body as my blood pumped through like race cars for the second time this day.

Our eyes locked again, but she sidestepped around me to get a plate, averting any awkward moment that was about to happen again.

I leafed through the tiny pockets of romaine and cheese and croutons and ranch while our elbows touched briefly with each reach. She smiled and laughed, and I wondered if she was on my level, thinking what I was thinking.

Doubtful.

"You can beat him," she said, eyeing her plate as she circled the ranch dressing around her romaine.

"What?" I asked, lost in the moment. I had left the Grant Hemingway talk at the table.

"You can beat him Grant Hemingway," she said, this time locking her brown eyes on me.

This time I heard her.

I could feel her words inside me, moving around, trying to find a couch to sit down on and make a home. This was the first time we had actually had a real conversation. Typically it never left the parking lot.

What kind of Gatorade do you like? Why are you running cross country? Have you taken Mr. Salisbury's class yet? Want to come to Abo's Pizza tonight with us?

"Well, he is, uh, pretty good," I stumbled. Not really wanting to talk about this anymore, but wanting to talk to her. "I'll have to, uh, figure it out, how to beat him."

She watched me intently as my eyes scanned my plate for the right words. Perhaps there's something in the slithers of cheese, or the pickle I placed on the side for dessert.

I stared into my salad the way a fortune teller stares into their crystal ball, only I wasn't really getting any insight from the contents on my plate. I was only creating an awkward moment.

"Well, if you believe you can, you will. And I believe in you," she said with a smile, eyes locked on mine. Her dark irises only made the whites around them all the more florescent. She flashed an inviting smile as she passed me and went back to booth.

What the hell was that?

6

OH, THE RANKINGS. . .

I LISTENED TO THE SMALL PEBBLES OF ROCK AND DIRT crunch beneath my Adidas Boosts. I ran between the pockets of shade along Mesa Trail alone, smelling the pine that lingered in the air. Tiny droplets of sweat flicked from my elbows as I danced along the rocks between Bear Peak and Green Mountain. That crisp morning was a little chilly in the shade. It hinted that autumn was somewhere around the corner.

On Colorado's Front Range you always got hints of the changing seasons in the mornings. There would be a slight bite in the air, not cold, but chilly. It'd prompt a warm up with long sleeves before ditching the additional clothes once you had enough body heat to sustain yourself the rest of the run without going into hypothermia.

You could not only see the beginnings of autumn in the trees, as they went from green to a light yellow or orange or red, but you could smell them changing. Looking at the landscape was like looking at a colorful canvas.

It was my favorite time of the year—it reminded me of my childhood on the east coast, where the landscape was saturated with trees. There would be year-round color, where soon the Front Range would be painted in beige until April.

But not yet.

I tried to focus on the jagged edges of the rocks, the birds chirping their hopeful morning song, *there's always hope in the morning*, the dirt beneath me that hadn't seen a footprint on this day yet, the gentle rolling waterfall to my right, anything but those damn rankings.

The latest state rankings were released every Monday morning, and as much as I didn't want to look, I had to. It was like passing a horrible accident on the highway, you don't want to see the bloodied, lifeless body in the passenger seat with a severed limb, but then again, you did.

I hated to know where I stood, but I also relished in it. I *had* to know. No matter how good or bad, I had to know where I stood, so I could change it if need be. And after getting trounced by Grant Hemingway at the stage races, I had to know what the genius minds of Colorado coaches thought of my performance and where I stood moving forward.

I knew I wouldn't be number one or even number two, but come on, it was only two miles, and the first race of the season, and I had just run my best set of mile repeats ever the same week.

I climbed farther up the trail between the two towering peaks. Green Mountain hid behind the trees while Bear Peak stood rocky and exposed to the south, a skeletal mountain that always begged to be pursued.

An ultra-runner once got pinned under a rock atop Bear Peak and lost a leg in the process. But, Boulder being Boulder, he wasn't the kind of runner to simply let the rock and lost limb stop him—he frequents the trail to the top still, mechanical limb and all.

Talk about not having an excuse to ever bail out—in Boulder the bar is always high. There are always those sorts of inspirational stories of people overcoming the odds. It really makes you feel mediocre after a while, especially if you have all your limbs and aren't winning races.

When I reached the meadow—the turnaround point —I stopped for a moment to stand on the rock that overlooked the open space to the south. It wasn't exactly a meadow, but I called it that more as a reference point. I slowed to a walk as I reached the rock and stood with my hands on my hips.

A year ago my father and I took a photo at this exact spot. I can still see his big smile, hiding his teeth, content with tired eyes. We had accomplished something worthy of a smile, worthy of being temporarily satisfied.

A lot changes over the course of a year.

I thought to an hour earlier when I scrolled—*scrolled* —down the latest rankings, *scrolled,* to find my name sitting not-so-contentedly at number six.

Really?

The coaches of the state really think I'm the sixth best guy in the state? Coach always insisted that I dismiss the rankings as just rankings, but I always have a hard time with looking at them as two-dimensional pieces of content.

"State is what matters," he'd say.

I could already hear him repeating this to me this

afternoon. He'd know I'd be pissed to see I wasn't even in the top five. He knew I was better than that, and so did I, but when the rest of the state doesn't think so, it's really hard to maintain some semblance of confidence.

"We'll prove them all wrong when it matters the most," he'd say.

And he was right. But still, *sixth?*

That's bullshit.

Grant Hemingway sat on top the rankings, and while he only beat me by four seconds, the genius rankings somehow assume there'd be four people between me and him.

Really?

Maybe it was all those damn push-ups he did.

I brooded back on the trail, down, back toward Boulder, back to NCAR where my car was parked, back to reality.

I hated and loved knowing where I stood. They were *just* rankings, but they were the acceptance of the community. It meant that people believed in you. And what I was finding out the hard way was that your entourage of believers started small, always.

I told myself I had a secret. Coach had a secret. *We* had a secret. And soon we'd share that secret with the rest of the state. They'd see then that I was better than sixth. And then they'd feel stupid, or so I imagined.

Or maybe I really am just that crazy. Maybe I'm the one who'll feel stupid at Penrose in two months when I'm swallowing dust that's being kicked up in the air by Grant Hemingway and a handful of others. Maybe I am just *mediocre.*

What if this is all for naught? And I'm not really

bound for big things? Maybe this is one of those things I just waste my time pursuing in high school, and really I'm supposed to be a professional jazz saxophonist.

I was all-state my freshman year.

The numbers don't lie. That's the most humbling thing about this sport. If you're good, you're good. You can't talk or charm your way to winning a race, you win the race by winning the race. It's what I've always loved so much about this sport—it's objectivity.

No.

All those miles this summer don't equal mediocrity. It can't. I put in the work, and I'll see the results.

I'll have to prove them all wrong.

I didn't run to the train tunnel and back at Rollinsville every Sunday this past summer to be sixth. I didn't light my lungs on fire running up Green Mountain every Wednesday to be sixth. I didn't give my teammates a two-minute head start on our Tuesday evening five-mile runs and chase them down at sub-6 clips to be sixth.

Screw the rankings. They're just rankings.

I leaned forward and let gravity pull me down, along with my pace. I ran on in frustration, letting it fuel my stride. The crunch beneath my feet picked up and the sweat flung from my elbows faster now. I could feel the effort in my quads as I bounded off my toes, down, down, down the path.

It's easy to run fast when you're running downhill, so I leaned more into my stride to keep the effort up. If I was going to be better than sixth, I'd have to really work for it.

I'd prove them wrong.

7

FOOD FOR THOUGHT

"She knows how to drive a stick, if you know what I mean," Blake said. "And the way her hair swayed back and forth each time she shifted gears, aw man, it was sooo hot."

"You're so full of shit," Todd shot back. His long, tentacle-like fingers stretched around his meatball sandwich, bits of which remained just to the side of his upper lip.

Saving it for later?

"Fine, don't believe me, but I know," Blake said, lifting his hands up by his shoulders in the universal "don't shoot" pose. His broad shoulders made the motion even bigger while his eyes cast downwards at the clean table, off to some imaginary target. "I know."

He went back to making his way through a soggy peanut butter and jelly sandwich, eating the small sandwich with both hands, while Todd shook his head in disagreement. The tiny little black curl of his hair hid his one arching eyebrow.

Random students were scuffling behind us with colorful trays between the tight rows of tables inside the high-ceilinged cafeteria which was alive in color and conversation. The lunch hour was always a time to let your hair down, figuratively as well as literally. White noise blanketed any details from being heard, which made it private, despite being public.

On the north side of the cafeteria was a long line of glass cases which held trophies won by Flatirons High spanning the past five decades. Tiny golden figurines topped various trophies etched with the event and the result. Only a handful were cross country related, given that Flatirons wasn't really known for its prowess on the course before the past few years, before Coach's tenure.

Only one from the past two decades was in the cases, and that was from last year's third-place team finish.

Winning a State title, with a team or as an individual, got you into the center stage of that glass case, lined with fake gold to make it look all the more important, photo and all. A year ago barely anyone outside the team knew my name or of my existence, but I was determined to get into that case, immortalized forever inside the walls so I could come back fat and old and see it and no one would recognize the bony teenage version of myself, including me. Then they'd all know my name.

Oh, to have such high hopes in life.

"I refuse to believe that Sherry Shrieves, church-twice-a-week Sherry Shrieves, would do that," Todd said.

"Well, you can refuse to believe the sky is blue, doesn't make it true." Blake took another big bite out of his sandwich and let the thought hang. He was always good at implying something without ever having to really say it. It was also his best defense—he could deny having ever said something, because he never did, he just implied.

Once he made out with a sophomore from his Spanish class in the back of his Nissan by the soccer fields. When she got wind of his boasts she threw a textbook at him for sharing the juicy details of their late-night tryst. He simply replied that he never said they made out, just that she had a "talented tongue," meaning she could speak Spanish really well.

She wasn't amused.

"I'm just sayin'," he went on, clearly inviting Todd's disgust. "That she knows how to drive stick."

"And I'm saying you're so full of shit," Todd repeated himself. "Her dad's a freakin' pastor!"

"What does that have to do with anything? Are you saying religious girls don't know how to drive stick?"

"No, but that's not what I'm saying!"

"Todd, *I am* just saying she knows how to drive a stick because I let her drive my Jeep up to Flagstaff Saturday night."

Todd pursed his lips and shook his head as if he had a dog in the fight. He didn't even like Sherry like that, but he liked arguing with Blake. It was a game to both of them, whether they admitted it or not, to hate each other. It was a rivalry that went off the cross country course, but perhaps started on it.

"You guys bicker like a married couple," I chimed in, my one contribution to the conversation. I enjoyed the fly-on-the-wall existence most days. I lived vicariously through Blake's sexual adventures, given that he always had a girl on tap, and I barely knew how to talk to one.

Blake cracked a smile while Todd looked off into the

distance, clearly still annoyed at something that really didn't matter. At that, Blake had to turn the knife a little more, just for kicks.

"You know those tight turns, left, right, left, right. You really have to navigate those tight turns, make sure you've got a good grip, make sure your hand doesn't slip, well, slip too much. And you have to get down to the really, really low gears, *if you know what I mean.*"

He cracked a sly smile at me, waiting for Todd's response.

"There you go again," Todd lifted his hand in disgust. "With that '*if you know what I mean*' bullshit."

Blake laughed while finishing up his sandwich, clearly satisfied in his ability to get under Todd's skin.

It wasn't that hard.

I watched the whole scene play out from behind my salad. Those crunchy romaine lettuce tips offering little more than hydration, but the ranch dressing was where I allowed myself some flavor, and the cheese sprinkled over the top with croutons.

Salad served on a plastic tray with a plastic fork sort of loses its touch, but with a tempo run looming just hours away, it was all that my stomach could handle. I was already all bound up with that pre-race anxiousness: *Every workout matters. Every workout is an opportunity to make gains, make gains on Grant Hemingway.*

"What's the workout today?" Blake turned my direction and the conversation away from his sexual escapades.

"Tempo run, five miles for you guys, six for me, I think," I said with a chunk of lettuce in my mouth. "Coach said no faster than 5:45s the first two miles, then we can get moving. He wants to make sure we finish the workout, not like last time where we all went out way too fast and died and had to cut a mile."

Blake's brown eyes turned serious as if being given his battle orders for the afternoon. And just minutes ago he was cracking jokes, but a five-mile tempo starting at 5:45 was no joke. It meant there was work to do.

He nodded and cleaned his hands from the jelly that lined his thumb.

"I wish I knew that before I ate the sandwich," he joked.

Todd, on the other hand, was unfazed. He wasn't listening—he was still stuck on the whole gear-shifting joke.

"Okay, Blake, how about this." Todd was regrouping, shifting his weight in his seat like a kid just waking up in the pew from an hour-long church session. "When I kick your ass in the tempo, you admit that you're full of shit."

"Damn, Todd, let it go, man!" Blake lifted his hands in the air again, innocent of all crimes, including but not limited to implying things.

"Oh, what? You're scared I'll do it?"

"No I'm not scared. Of you? *Please.*"

"Then bet."

"Todd, I'll even up the ante and make it easy for you," Blake said, turning to face him. "I'll give you a thirty-second cushion, *if you know what I mean.*"

Todd turned his head and glared at Blake for a hard ten seconds before replying, "Oh you're sooo on."

"Settled, then? Half-minute man."

"That's not what your mom said last night," Todd shot back. "She was satisfied."

"Were you peeking through my parents' window?

Todd, you're a sick dude." Blake took it in stride. "You know, you could get arrested for peeping. That's a really serious thing to admit to. You should really seek treatment before someone busts you. I think I'm going to start calling you Peeping Todd instead of One-Step Todd."

It didn't matter how hard Todd tried to get that one step up on Blake like he did during the warm-ups, it just wasn't ever in the cards.

"Whatever, man, it's settled." Todd shook his head, throwing up the white flag in temporary defeat. "You're so dumb."

Three hours later Blake torched Todd by forty-six seconds, and I ran my fastest six-mile tempo ever—33:02.

And that was just the beginning.

8
___

THE STAMPEDE

FROM THE GROUND LEVEL AT PENROSE YOU CAN'T
exactly see the top of Pikes Peak—Cheyenne Mountain
stands in its way, but it's there, hiding behind another
object the way the Flatirons do when a low-lying cloud
rolls through early in the morning.

Down where the mortals live and eat and breathe at
6,119 feet, bodies were hurtling back and forth along the
rocky open space just to the south side of the Penrose
Stadium—the starting line.

It would be our first 5k of the season, though the
additional mile didn't exactly mean much—it was what
we had been training for all summer. What meant something on this day was the fact that we'd have our first run
on the State course. The only difference would maybe be
the thirty or so degrees cooler it could be in two months,
or it could be in the upper seventies like this morning. A
Colorado Front Range autumn has many cards.

I bounced up and down on the starting line to get my
calves nice and warm while my teammates and nearly

everyone else sprinted out into the open space in front of us.

The Penrose course, when it served as the Colorado State course, was unique in the sense that we didn't start or end on grass—we barely ran on grass. The start was a dirt rodeo grounds parking lot with too many rocks. This made the spike choice all the more important. Something with a plastic plate, like my favorite Zoom Kennedys, would be a no-go here. You wanted something with a rubber bottom, and not too long of spikes, because just 200 meters into the race the course hit pavement for a bit. Once out, away from all the horse shit, the course rolled over more traditional Front Range terrain with mountainous views to the west, the kind of stuff tourists love to see. That's where you could call this a "cross country course," because there was grass. Some, at least. The final mile brought you back to the rodeo grounds, up a dirt hill with too many big rocks, and into the stadium where the grounds were clean, yes, but it was hard not to think of all the random animals that defecated on the dirt we'd share our spikes with in the fall.

I've never been one to clean my spikes—I prefer the battle to remain on them—but it did make it a bit more challenging when screwing in my spikes.

Nevertheless, I bounded with a mixture of fatigue and anxiousness in my legs. I was eager to get this shindig on the road, but also tired from that tempo earlier in the week.

Coach was quick to remind me, and all of us, that all that mattered today was feeling out the course. We needed to see it. We'd most likely be tired, yes, but that was okay—it was November that mattered, not the end of August.

Still, I was 0-1 on the season and searching for my first big win.

There would be no Grant Hemingway on the starting line of this one, which made me breathe a little easier, though Dakota Ridge's Vince Charles was a threat.

Vince was one of those guys who was good all throughout high school. He won the prestigious "Head of the Class" award his freshmen and sophomore year. The only runner in the class to beat him as a junior was me. Despite this fact, I knew I couldn't count him out—he always indulged in the mediocrity within the distance events of late-summer track, meaning he had some legit speed early on in the cross country season. And, he's Vince Charles, he's always good.

Vince stood a stout 5'8" and looked more like a wrestler than a runner. He had piercing light blue eyes and a sly smile that he had perfected from years of newspaper interviews—he was quite familiar with being the center of attention. I envied his savvy answers every time I read them in the paper. He wasn't nearly as awkward as me. I envisioned him a future CEO of some tech company, or perhaps something within natural foods. He was cool and collected, and he stood just twenty meters to my left, leaning into the start while the gun raised high in the air.

"Racers, take your marks!"

Words that always made me cringe, as much as loved to hear them, which seems to be the trend with everything running-related. We indulge in a sport that causes pain, and yet the more of it we seek, the faster we run. It's a hate/love relationship, and it's the only kind I've ever been in.

"Set!"

Another one of those moments I love to hate.

And then 200 boys storm the field. I imagine this is what war was like back before it became so industrialized. Just a bunch of young boys who have no idea what the hell they're getting themselves into, running out—*out*—because someone else said so.

Add a first 5k of the season to nearly everyone's head, and you've got one insanely hot pace.

While everyone was sprinting at nearly top speed, I hovered behind the lead, eyeing the two bicyclists with a smile: David Car and Lucent McDonald.

I shared nearly half my summer mileage with David and Lucent before they went off to college at Pine Creek, an NAIA school just outside Colorado Springs that was hosting the Stampede. When I got word that they'd be the lead bikers, my mind calmed ever so slightly, knowing that if everything went well, the latter stages of this race would be a lot like my summer mileage: the three of us hammering along the trails.

After cruising through the opening mile just over five minutes in a pack of nearly half a dozen I felt the itch to put my stamp on the race. Along with sharing some sweat with David and Lucent in the summer, I was glued to the Tour de France and felt some urge to adopt road cycling style to cross country, like at the stage races.

Bikers don't surge gradually, they take off. They attack. They take the field by surprise. And if they're successful, the surprise attack works and they pedal off to victory. Taking that and bringing it to the course seemed *creative*.

Be an artist—do something different.

I moved outside and threw down the hammer like a runner kicking the final lap of a mile race on the track.

No one came with.

No one even attempted to jump on the train—with good reason. I dropped a 32-second 200 off and away, and was determined to keep the pace hot until I didn't have a negotiable shadow.

I hammered my way up the long gradual hill after the mile marker with Bear Creek down below, chasing David and Lucent, who had to jump up from their seats and onto the pedals to stay in front of me, dancing on the pedals like climbers.

Off to the quiet section of the course there was very little encouragement from the crowd, meaning anyone wishing to chase would have to do so without any help. This was strategic.

David and Lucent took frequent glances back to check my progress and offered "Keep rolling, Baxter!" a few times in hushed tones since technically they weren't supposed to be cheering or helping anyone, but when you share a few hundred miles of sweat on the trails, you're practically brothers.

I ran on in the silence, which was reminiscent of those summer miles that no one sees but only you feel. Behind me a chase was forming, but I didn't think much on that. I focused ahead and tried to envision the State meet, and how ideal this scenario would be: running freely up front without a challenging shadow in sight.

I leaned down the long gradual hill past the two-mile and began to feel the effort in my legs a bit. I could see the stadium and hear cheers off in the distance, and soon they'd be roaring as I made my way through the tunnel of painted bodies and parents with cameras back near the creek crossing.

By the third mile I was running scared. The pace and heat were beginning to take their toll, and I knew Vince and others had to be catching me now. My arms swayed from side to side rather than back and forth, and I leaned forward in desperation, a car quickly running out of gas.

David and Lucent continued to give quiet cheers, though when they went silent I knew someone was coming. I knew my time in the spotlight up front was running out. Now the only question was could I outlast whoever it was? Would my chaser run out of real estate? Or would they time it just right?

Finally en route back toward the creek crossing where everyone would be standing along the bridge I threw in what was remaining in my tank. There were nearly 600 meters between me and potentially my first win, but based on the cheers I knew I wasn't safe.

I once was the predator, attacking the field so damn early at the mile, now I was the prey, being stalked by an unknown predator, and me too afraid to turn and look— the ultimate white flag.

Never glance back—it'll give your challengers reason to believe you're dying; it'll give them motivation to continue their pursuit of pain and pride.

I took two massive leaps through the creek, getting my spikes wet—the reason I ditched wearing socks last year—which added weight. I could hear a splash just a few seconds after me.

I pumped hard up the double hill, the second of which was insanely steep and a lot like the hill back on our loop in Boulder. If you could survive this, you'd make it to the finish in one piece, or so I told myself.

I could hear cheers beyond the fronts of the crowds, nameless people in the colors, the white noise of all the pain and chaos of a cross country meet.

"Go Baxter!"

I didn't know who they were, but I could hear them.

My lungs joined the pain party with my legs and arms, and I could feel the stiffness crawling up my back. Every step brought me closer to the stadium where we'd take a sharp right and there'd be a clear pathway to the finish. I was in the red now.

One more turn and I'd be able to see it: the finish line. I couldn't think of State now, or anything else beyond the next step, because *everything* hurt.

And then it happened.

Right as I cut inwards to take that one last turn into the stadium I saw a flash of something fly by me on my left. It happened so fast I couldn't even make out who it was. Whoever it was was in an entirely other gear.

There'd be no battle to the finish on this one, because that jerk was kicking the final 100 like a JV kid cracking 25 for the first time. He made me look like I was standing still.

Defeated, I galloped in while the crowd cheered a sprinter version of Vince Charles on into victory. I had the not-so-welcoming view of watching him part the tape from a few seconds back, his spiked feet high behind him, sweat dripping down his white skin.

At least I made him work for it.

Oh, so close.

I crossed three seconds after him, simply amazed at how much he destroyed me over the final 100 meters.

Who does that?

After crossing the line a clear second—third was nowhere to be seen—I slowed to walk and patted Vince on the back while he sucked sweet oxygen with his hands on his knees.

This. Will. Not. Happen. Again.

Despite the pain which still lingered, my mind was already busy cursing itself out. Zero and two on the season, a season in which I hoped to win a State title.

And I just lost on the State course.

But hey, at least I earned a t-shirt for placing in the top ten.

A year ago that would've made my day. Now, it stung. A reminder of how I went out too hard too early and got kicked down right when I took the last turn. I even had a glimpse of an unimpeded finish line *for a brief second.*

Oh, so close.

9

STROLLING DOWN PEARL

I COULDN'T HEAR A WORD LILY WAS SAYING, BUT I watched her mouth as she ordered something from the man on the other side of the tall counter at the ice cream shop off Pearl Street. She spoke quietly, gesturing with her hands, and her big brown eyes were locked on her subject. She had the sort of gaze you locked with, but it scared the hell out of you because you could feel her reading your mind.

The man on the other side nodded underneath his company hat, clearly feeling her vibes as well. I envied him for having her attention in that moment but then remembered that she was there with me.

This wasn't a date, or so I was telling myself. It was. . . a meet up? I didn't want to jump to any conclusions that might scare her off, so I downplayed the event, even if it was just us two. Lily seemed like the kind of person that didn't really cling to definitions. She was more into being wherever she was at the moment and perhaps defining it later. While this ran contrary to the way I went about things, there was something about it that drew me in, like a challenge.

After our Saturday night post-meet tradition of Abo's, Lily asked if I was headed home or staying out a little longer since I had a few more hours left on my midnight curfew. I didn't exactly have anything else to do. Typically I'd head home and read while downing a bag of purple Skittles and a cream soda from the gas station, like all cool kids on a Saturday night in Boulder.

When I did want to stay out, I'd head to the Lighthouse Bookstore off Pearl and scan the aisles for something to read. I'd stroll up and down, eyeing the wooden shelves, waiting for a book to reach out to me: *read me.* Blake always gave me shit for this, but I swear, listening for a book to speak to me almost always led to a great read. I found Jack Kerouac's *On the Road* in this manner, and I couldn't put that one down.

Add that the book store was right next door to an ice cream shop, and it seemed like destiny.

Lily had a tiny cone in her hand topped with a variety of colors that looked delicious. I held the double door open so we could stroll down Pearl Street like tourists. The four-block red-brick road is one of the hot spots for people who don't exactly live in Boulder, and while it's typically overrun with people taking too many photos and stopping every few feet to stare at the entertainers begging for money, it's iconic Boulder in nearly every way.

There are the dive bars down a few dark stairs right next door to over-priced restaurants where you can get an eight-ounce steak for $60.

There are colorful and meticulously planted flowers

and dirty alleyways where public pissing is a thing on a late Saturday night.

There are high-end clothing stores with homeless bums outside with their cardboard signs asking for money. A third of them are likely college dropouts living off their parents' trust fund. Another third own homes outside the bubble and do this for money. The rest truly are homeless and smart enough to take advantage of someone who looks at a $20 bill like most look at a penny.

It's rich and poor simultaneously, and somewhere in the middle are the book shops and coffee stops. It's an overload of the senses, but when Lily Bissinger hints that she'd like to hang out a little longer, you go. The windows of opportunity don't open often, or at least since I've known her. Her confidence was insanely attractive, and when she gave you the microphone to speak, she made you feel like the only one in the room. She was some sort of a seductive mystery to me.

We walked down the red brick road between tourists taking photos, which I'm sure we made the background of. I always wanted to turn and pose quickly in the back of someone's photos, hoping they wouldn't catch it until later, after they'd printed it out and canvased it in their house. Then they'd see a lanky tan kid in the back smiling with two thumbs up.

Lily worked on her cone though those brown eyes were locked on me. It was nerve-wracking. We walked just a foot apart along the busy sidewalk, her left hand dangling just inches from my right hand, which was already sweating in anxiousness.

"Why do you do this?" She broke the silence between

licks from her cone, her eyes darting between me and her ice cream. Those big brown eyes like traffic lights, directing the way of attention.

"Do what?"

"Run?"

"What do you mean?"

"You didn't just join the team like most of us. You're like, *really* into it."

"Is that a bad thing?" I said.

"No," she explained. "I guess I was just curious how or why you got into it, because you seem to really enjoy it. I think it's really cool."

"Uh, okay. Are you, uh, sure you want to go down this road?"

Her brown eyes looked almost hazel when she looked up from her cone. The sun was just setting over the mountains to the west, sending a streak down Pearl Street and on Lily's face. She licked her cone down to the core while her forehead wrinkled slightly in thought. "Sure."

"Well, I actually started running when my dad got sick a few years back," I started. "He was in the hospital for, like, almost a year. He almost died."

We walked on and I tried to avoid locking eyes with her. The tiny wrinkles in her forehead told me she was still interested. We lingered in the silence for bit, which made me feel like I needed to keep talking, like I hadn't fully answered her question yet.

"My sister was away in college. Mom was tending to him half the time, working the other half, and taking care of me. She did a lot. So I was at home a lot alone, and I started running, because I had all this pent-up energy. I had nothing else to do. So I'd go out and run around on the trails. It just felt good, you know? It was an outlet."

She nodded along, though something told me she hadn't experienced any real trauma in her life, at least not yet. Or maybe I was just jumping to conclusions based on her non-responses. She always was hard to read, and that made me want to read her all the more.

"And then, I don't know. . . you do something enough and you get better at it. I just sort of got good over time, then by the time he got released I just made varsity. He wanted to come to every race. The better I got, the more excited he was, like, it was something he could brag about to his friends. So I guess I got more into it because he was."

Our hands dangled closer, but now my mind was elsewhere, somewhere in the past.

"What was he sick from?" she asked.

"Leukemia."

We walked on in silence for a moment while my mind raced, replaying the events of the past four years. For the first time all night I wasn't in a trance over her. She had asked me something, something deep, that for once took my attention off her gaze, off her, and beyond to something out there in the abyss. I hadn't really traced my steps until she asked that question.

"He lost a ton of weight. I'd never seen him so fragile in my entire life. He was always like a god to me, this big strong man, and then he got sick, and he could barely walk to the bathroom without help. It was surreal. I think it was the first time I realized he was mortal."

10

BOLD DREAMS

THE FRESHLY CUT GRASS TINGLED THE BOTTOMS OF my feet.

I cruised over the surface at just under seven minutes a mile around the inside of the bright red track at Flatirons High while the vibrant autumn sun beamed bright overhead. It had become common to run the last mile of most of our runs that ended at the track barefoot so we could strengthen the feet, but for me, it was more about the sensation of running barefoot on the grass. It felt pure, natural, *freeing*.

Sure, my feet would be stained dark green after this, but the feeling itself made running all the more pleasurable. If I could find miles worth of cut grass, I'd run barefoot all the time. If I could sneak onto a golf course before anyone teed off, I'd run the whole thing barefoot.

Coach ran alongside me, as he often did on the tail end of typical mileage days. Nearly everyone else on the team had already completed their quota for the day, though I always had a few extra miles on my plate. His mechanical movements contrasted against my loose stride, which mirrored my lanky frame. Since I was tall everything I did appeared lanky or needed the word applied to it.

"Feeling good?" he asked between breaths.

"Yeah, I feel like I've got more pop in my stride this week."

"Good, good. Let's make sure to get in some strides after this, and then again Thursday and Friday so you'll be feeling a little sharper Saturday."

"Sounds good. Have you heard the new Weezer album yet?"

"Not yet. Is it good?"

"Oh, man, Coach, it's really good! I won't ruin it for you."

He was an ideal training partner. We usually passed the time talking about racing or training, but on longer days we'd dive into music. Pearl Jam. Weezer. The Smashing Pumpkins (his favorite). Radiohead. We were unheard musical critics who had an opinion about everything.

"I still think the *Blue* album is their best one."

"Better than the *Green* album? Better than *Pinkerton*?"

"Don't get me started, Coach."

The only times we ran more than a cool down mile together was during the off-season, which was when I really got to know him a few years back.

It was the winter of my sophomore year when he caught me passing his room in my running clothes, headed out for a dreary and lonely six mile run when he told me to wait up.

We were just a few weeks beyond the end of the cross

country season, which was capped with a fifty-fourth place finish at State for me, and a twelfth place team finish. It was the end of Coach's first season at Flatirons as well as mine. As a transfer, I still hadn't made any friends, which meant running the winter miles solo.

But not on this day.

We sloshed along the wet trails down South Boulder Creek while trickles of rain fell from the sky. The Flatirons loomed in the distance but hid within the low-lying clouds. My shirt was already soaked and weighing me down, but I didn't mind so much. I'd had no company on a run like this in the past month, and already Coach was making it easier.

We talked about the season behind us and how I was disappointed with how it ended.

"I want to be better than this," I brooded. "There were eleven sophomores and four freshmen who ran faster than me in the state this year."

Coach listened like a psychiatrist to my complaints and gave his two cents between my musings.

"I think the longer runs on Sundays will really help this winter, and if we keep up on plyometrics twice a week and strides three times a week, I'm thinking we'll start seeing some big improvements. It's just going take time."

What I had come to admire in Coach was that he never prescribed something he himself wouldn't do or likely hadn't already done. When he'd say, "One more 400 repeat," it's because he knew the mental toll of having to get up for one more when you thought you were done—because he had experienced it himself as an athlete. It was this fact that made his advice all the more sought out.

"Let's break this down, season by season, year by year," he said. "Let's talk goals."

We ran on in the rain while I listed my projections and desires for the next year and a half before stopping on my senior year, the grand finale, the curtain call, the last-ditch effort to leave my mark as a Somebody. Coach listened intently, taking mental notes of everything I was saying while he ran alongside this younger, more ignorant version of me.

"Okay, so sub 10 your junior year in the 3200, and sub 4:40 in the mile. Sounds good. Now, senior year."

"I want to win."

"County? Region? State?"

"All of them."

We ran on in silence for a minute while Coach presumably pondered how he could be running next to such an overly ambitious lunatic with no grasp on reality. I had to have sounded crazy. Here was a kid who just finished fifty-fourth at State his sophomore year, and he was talking about *winning* the big dance in two years. I didn't know it at the time, but in that moment, I was self-assured that it would happen, or could, at least. Given some miracle. I hadn't yet understood how easy it was to talk of such ambitious goals and how hard it would actually be to achieve them.

"Well," he broke the silence. "We've got some work to do. Those are some pretty bold dreams, but if we work hard, stick to the plan, we can make it happen."

Nearly two years later we were once again striding side by side, this time with the first big test on tap: County was set for Saturday, and I was entering as the underdog.

11

COUNTY

Lyons is a small town nestled in the gateway to the Rocky Mountains off Highway 36. It's surrounded on all sides by steep cliffs, exposing Colorado's vast history. Slicing straight through the middle of town is the mighty St. Vrain River, which cuts through the mountains like a butter knife.

Despite being a town of just over 2,000 people, Lyons is home to one of the most storied small-school programs in Colorado history.

For years they've dominated the 2A landscape, and not with runners who can only compete in the small school divisions, but titans that put big-school kids to shame. Okay, maybe that last line was a little harsh, but Lyons consistently has athletes who can compete on the big stage—maybe that's the nicer way to put it.

At the helm of the program has been Greg Marks, who is a prominent figure in the community and the state. He's assertive and bold, and almost always right. You can question him all you want about anything, but he's almost always got an answer, and it's based on reality. Life is simplified.

Marks has led his team to too many State titles to count, and among them were his own children, each of whom has a handful of titles to battle their siblings with. Spanning well over a decade, the name Marks appears among the winners of a State title over thirty times, whether that be his eldest son John, his daughter Sarah, his middle child Michael, his youngest daughter Mary, or his youngest son Gabriel, who was the last of the family to storm through the Colorado high school cross country and track scene, which is currently enjoying a void between Marks children. Since he has no more children, a doorway has opened, though not for long—his children now have children of their own, and per the trend, they're already blazing around the roads of Colorado.

This gap in Marks-family dominance created an opportunity for someone with a different name to shine at Lyons, and Coach Marks knew how to foster such talents. While I never got to race a Marks, that year featured someone just as threatening: Christian Mayer.

Christian is one of those soccer-turned-runner talents, like Blake. He would run thirty-mile weeks and still run over the competition before Coach Marks got a hold of him. Since Marks had him training year-round, he was the classic Lyons star, able to compete in 5A and dominate 2A.

Add that Christian was a three-time State champ—winning as a freshman—and owner of the course record at Lyons, which is where County was that year. I entered the meet as a clear underdog, which was a persona I was quickly taking on.

But there's something appealing about that fact.

It gave me the opportunity to create my own attack, knowing that Christian would be on the defense—he had more to lose. Senior year, hadn't won a County title yet (since it encompassed the big schools like Fairview, Boulder, and Niwot), but a star in his own right among the smaller schools. This could be his only shot at claiming a title that would distinguish him as the best runner in the entire state, given that he'd be up against the big schools, like Flatirons. It was his home course, which he held the record on.

I could use that and turn it on him.

So Coach and I devised *The Plan*.

The course sat on a gentle slope on the south side of the town. It included an uphill start that climbed gradually for nearly 600 meters before flattening out—temporarily. For every mile, there were at least two hills to climb. It was perhaps the toughest, or one of the toughest, courses in the state. The two-loop course provided an opportunity to gauge where everyone else was and strategize an attack. The second loop of the course was typically where everyone dropped like flies—the double hill just after the mile-and-a-half marker seemed like an optimal spot to attack, but not the bottom of the hill—he'd expect that.

So *The Plan* was to run within the lead pack for a mile, then disguise a surge by running one step ahead of Christian and the pack. He'd think this was *The Move*, and counter it by letting me lead, thinking this race was already over with him winning it. I'd remain there, one step ahead, until the double hill, where'd I'd once again mask a surge with a fake one at the bottom, barely upping the pace, then, halfway up the hill when he thought he had me and was about to make a surge of his own, I would attack. All chips in. Sprint to the finish. Game Over. Done. Kaput.

The plan, essentially, was to use his advantages against him. If I could make him think he had me, his guard would come down ever so slightly, and I'd have the advantage of surprise, which was perhaps the only real way I could beat him: *strategically.*

We had previewed the course the previous week and established *The Plan,* leaving no detail to chance.

"This will be *your* big day," Coach said the night before. "Like you said your sophomore year, you want to win County, now it's here. Let's do this."

I could sense the anxiousness in his voice, but I was in the same boat. There was talking about doing big things, and then there was actually doing them. And now, it was time to quit talking and start doing.

Anyone could have bold dreams, but making them become reality was an entirely different game, as I had come to realize in the past month.

But I was determined not to be one of the many who talk big and can't deliver. No. That just wasn't my style, and here was the opportunity to prove it. If I could beat Christian Mayer on his home course senior year, I could be *somebody.* Then I'd have to be considered better than sixth in the state, per the latest set of rankings.

Winning here would mean I was legit. It would mean I had a shot of taking down Grant Hemingway next month.

So naturally, I couldn't eat breakfast the morning of the race. My stomach was tied in knots, knowing a secret that no one else did, except for Coach. This would be the day we'd hint at what was about to come in another. The day my single would drop and everyone would be like *"Damn! That shit is hot!"*

In my alternate life I'm a rapper with gold teeth and a platinum album hanging on my bedroom wall next to the print-out of my latest goal written in bold: **"WIN COUNTY."**

The sun peeked between the sharp ridges to the east, drying portions of the course, though much of the thick grass remained wet with dew. I didn't care. It didn't matter what the variable, I had simplified the process enough to know one thing: I would win this race.

The flashes of colors and scents didn't distract me one bit, as much as I wanted to be distracted, just to ease the tension a little. Not today.

I envisioned this as a precursor to State. Beating Christian would give me the confidence that I could beat Grant Hemingway. Because if I couldn't beat the 2A State champ, how could I beat the best—*currently*—in 5A?

On the starting line I kept a watchful eye on Christian, looking for signs of nervousness. He knew the stakes just as I did, only he had the weight of expectations on his shoulders. I only had the weight of my secret.

I jumped off the line in a few quick strides, getting a feel for the grass beneath my spikes. Back on the starting line Christian was doing push-ups, which seemed odd to me—who does push-ups before a race?

Nevertheless, there was work to be done.

"Back the line, gentlemen!" Marks said in a booming voice with the starter's gun in his hand. He was always so prompt, so decisive.

The 200 bodies jogged back to the line, shaking out their limbs, trying to ease the nerves, unsuccessfully of course.

In the quiet of the moment I thought to myself of that run with Coach two years before, and to our conversation the night before. *This was it.* Time to do or die.

It'll all be different after this, I told myself. The secret won't be one anymore.

"To your marks." The gun went up, and we all leaned slightly down, ready to explode off the line.

Smoke in the air.

Eight minutes later I found myself flying down the steep hill just before the two mile with Christian chasing about forty meters back. It was like I went to sleep for half the race and just now woke up to find myself leading it.

Where did the time go?

The race was unfolding into my hands just the way Coach and I planned—*when does that ever happen?*

After the initial attack on cue, I sprinted by a reporter for the *Daily Camera* who whispered, "Don't go too early" when I passed. I couldn't tell if he was saying that with hopes I'd win, or doubting that I could sustain the pace.

Regardless, it only added fuel to my fire.

I cruised by the track and into the final lap without fear and spite fueling every stride. I'd take whatever I could get at this point, because Christian was stalking or holding on, I couldn't tell, somewhere behind me. I didn't feel safe, and I wouldn't for another five minutes.

Back down and around the open field where the start was, I powered on, feeling heavy from the effort. I waited for Christian to roll me up, but with each stride, he didn't.

Where the hell was he?

When does anything ever go according to plan?

I pumped my arms up the long gradual hill one more time, striding ever so closer to the finish.

Eight hundred to go and I still didn't see any shadows, but I could still feel his presence.

He must be waiting to kick.

No. No. Not this late. You don't come this far and lose it this late. Not. Anymore.

I could hear the crowd in the distance now, waiting for us to come kicking in. The hometown hoping it was their boy, and the rest of the crowd hoping for someone new. *Me, perhaps?*

With 400 to go I stormed through the opening in the woods and down the narrow path to the track where it'd all open up. I couldn't lose it here now. That'd be a travesty and so embarrassing for it to happen *again*. I pumped my arms harder and leaned into the downhill. If I could just get to the opening without Christian on my shoulder, I knew I could pull it off.

Upset City.

My shoulders went tight and I struggled to keep my eyes open as the pain increased. Down and down I went and then the light. Out from the tunnel of trees I could see the beautiful sight of the finish line, and colorful crowds on both sides leading me in.

And then—the gasp, followed by my father's raspy scream. "Go Baxter!" His words echoed across the open field and were followed by my mother's high pitched scream.

The white noise turned to a roar as I crossed the track in full sprint and tore across the grass to the finish. Christian was somewhere behind me now, but I could sense by the cheers of the crowd the race was over. He would not be catching me on this day. But still, fear fueled my stride —the bitter taste of being out-kicked by Vince Charles was still very much in my mouth, and I wanted nothing more than to cleanse that shit out.

This would do.

I felt the tunnel to the finish tighten just before the line and the crescendo crashed as I crossed the line in 15:54.

I slowed to a walk, wide-eyed, trying to process what just happened.

Did I just win County?

A boy in a t-shirt two sizes too big handed me a medal with "1" on the back. I didn't care for it. My first thought was "You can keep that."

But he insisted.

I walked out from between the lined finishing area, still in a shock. I turned around just to confirm that I had won the race. Behind me, just beyond the finish line, I saw the figure of Christian Mayer on his hands and knees, defeated.

Did that just happen?

As more runners trickled in I paused by the fence to watch, still unsure of the moment.

Was this a dream?

And then it hit me.

Coach came sprinting over, arms wide with a big smile on his face.

"You did it!" he screamed, followed by half the JV and a slew of parents and people I had never seen in my entire life.

Soon there were journalists with pens and pads and cameras lingering, waiting for me to catch my breath.

I didn't know what to do. Or where to go.

All I knew was that I was one third of the way there, and with a new course record.

PART II

12

EXPOSED

L<small>IFE WAS A LITTLE DIFFERENT WALKING THROUGH</small>
the halls of Flatirons High Monday morning. And when I
say a little, I mean a lot. It was like I had a blinking neon
sign around my neck saying "Look at me!" Kids stole
glances while I wondered if I had breakfast still dripping
from my chin or on my shirt. Perhaps a stream of toilet
paper flowing from the backs of my pleated khakis. *I was
wearing pants—right?*

It likely had to do with the fact that the *Daily Camera*
sports section included a massive photo of my pained
face, clearly not my most photogenic moment. I mean,
not the kind a girl is going to look at and be like "Wow,
he's hot." No. This was more likely to do the opposite.
The headline read in bold lettering, "Reeves is the Real
Deal" and included a few stumbling quotes from me that
clearly showed I was still somewhat confused as to what
just happened.

While it wasn't the kind of thing to prompt a girl to
really talk to me, I mean come on, the photo painted me

with big breathing nostrils searching for air, my mouth a gigantic abyss like I had just eaten something I was about to puke up, and my wild dark eyes looking like I was about to set fire to a tricycle like Firestarter.

The Look of Death.

It was the kind of thing that would spark the interest of the father or the mother, however. A stud runner at the local school? How nice. Good thing we pay taxes here, maybe it'll increase the value of our home, since the school is getting good at a lot of stuff.

Perhaps I could win a girl desiring her parents' affections, who, upon hearing her father or mother rave about the kid in school who won County, would be interested.

Who said Mommy and Daddy issues were a bad thing?

Even in the classroom, it was weird.

Mrs. Blake started the day congratulating me in front of the class. She had me stand up, and put her petite tan hands on my shoulders.

Yes, Mrs. Blake. . .

I stood awkward next to the white marker board and heard her say how the most exciting part of her Sunday was opening the sports pages to see one of her students gracing the cover, ugly photo and all. I didn't have to the guts to say that her acknowledging my presence just made my day, though I'm sure my reddening cheeks said enough. In that one moment, I was getting what nearly every other boy in class wanted: *Mrs. Blake's attention.*

It was like that everywhere.

Everyone wanted to know about the race, even though they already knew.

"What was it like to win?"

"When did you break away from that fast dude?"

"Did you get a medal?"

"What are you doing Friday night?"

"Saturday night?"

"Got a date for Homecoming yet?"

"What is it like to be on the cover of the sports section?"

Immortalized wooden pulp.

Even my parents were a little star-struck. My mother neatly cut out the photos and story and placed a magnet over it on the fridge, something she had done when my sister frequented the paper, which was often back in the day. My father had something to brag about to his coworkers.

Now I wasn't just their son, they were *my* parents. *Baxter's parents.* The scope of attention had shifted in the span of fifteen minutes and fifty-four seconds.

A week ago I wasn't known outside the team, and barely outside my house, and now I had random girls and guys congratulating me as I walked to lunch. I didn't really know what to say or what to do. I just knew I wanted to be around someone I could talk to, rather than answer more questions about the same race.

Cue: Lily.

She came around the corner and into the lunch room with her light brown curls flowing and the scent of lilac drifting from her shoulders, books clutched tight to her chest. She wore a light orange blouse with ruffles on the shoulders, exposing her lightly tanned skin.

"Oh, hey, Mr. Big Shot," she said with a smile and those beaming brown eyes. "I was going to send a special announcement over the intercom, or write a note in bright red lipstick over your windshield with a heart and my number, or make a giant billboard for your yard saying 'Congrats!' but I think everyone else beat me to the punch."

"Please don't do that," I said, shaking my head and walking alongside her. "Most of these people didn't even know I went to their school Friday. Now Monday all of sudden they want to be my friend."

"Don't be so lame, Baxter," she shot back, glaring at me. "Don't be that kid who gets attention for something he did and then shy away from it because he can't handle it."

"I'm not saying that I—"

"I'll start calling you Kurt Cobain if you do that."

"Don't do that."

"Or J.D. Salinger."

"Don't do that."

"Do you know any other recluses?"

"I'm not saying that," I repeated. "It's just. . . *weird*."

Lily shot me a glance with those big brown eyes and tiny wrinkles in her forehead that made my knees weak.

Oh, to be inside her head right now.

"Okay, Mr. Big Shot," she said, averting her eyes back to the masses of color in front of us. "Where will his royal highness like to sit?"

"Oh, come on, Lily, don't do that."

"I'm just messing with you," she said with a laugh. "You've got to lighten up. It's just County."

"Ouch."

"I didn't mean it like that," she back pedaled. "I just meant that it's not State."

"I'm well aware of that fact."

"So lighten up." She shrugged and led the way through the walking, talking bodies toward the far table by the window, somewhere near the exit, per my suggestion. I needed to be near fresh air, somewhere where I could escape if need be. The world already felt smaller, and it was barely noon on Monday.

"I'm just saying," she continued once we could sit within earshot of each other, "is that you can't let all of this get to you."

She motioned her hands to the crowd sitting in the lunch room behind me. I sat with my back to the room, not wanting to make eye contact with anyone. Her fingernails were painted a light purple.

"I know, it's just weird," I tried to explain. "It's like being exposed a little, or a lot."

"Then don't win the race," she shot back, eyes wide with her eyebrows climbing upwards. There was no winning any conversation with her. She was always a step ahead.

"No, I don't mean it's like. . ." I searched for the words floating somewhere up in my head, something to explain myself. "On the course, I don't mind. It's my world, or it feels that way. I'm comfortable with the spotlight on the course, or on Saturday mornings, it's part of winning, or being near the front, having an impact on the race. But in school or anywhere else, it's weird. It's a different world, so it feels weird when they converge. It makes sense for people to care about running when you're at a meet, but when you're walking down the hall or sitting in English, it's. . . weird. People ask too many questions."

"Like?" She pried for more while she unpacked her lunch one item at a time. A neatly sliced sandwich cut diagonally, a miniature sized bag of Fritos, and a blue Gatorade.

"Like 'Why did you start running in the first place?'" I shot back with a pixie grin, trying to once again divert from any real conversation.

13

SETBACK

THE PARTY ON TOP OF THE MOUNTAIN WAS SHORT-lived. A week later I got my ass handed to me. I wasn't second, or third, or even fourth at Liberty Bell—the fastest course in the state. I was fifth and never really in the race.

I threw in what I was deeming my trademark attack halfway through the race, but this time there was no shifting of gears, only a stall out on the highway.

Christian Mayer had his revenge, along with a few others. I watched from the bottom of the hill while he sprinted up in racing flats, arms wide with likely a big smile—I couldn't see it—because I was six seconds back. It was the first time of the season I entered the final straightaway clearly out of the race. Six seconds doesn't sound like much, but when you've got four guys in front of you, and you're already running at top gear, it's demoralizing.

It might as well be a minute.

"Don't worry," Coach said after the race, though I

could see the worry in his eyes. He didn't smile, and he tried to explain to me, as well as himself, that this was part of the process. "We just introduced the half-mile hill repeats—those are bound to put some heaviness in your legs. Remember, we want State—that's the only race that matters."

I nodded along but his words didn't stick as much as they needed to. A loss was a loss, and after last week's big win, this one stung. I thought I had already crossed this river. I was hoping to skate on to State with a streak in my back pocket.

Setback.

What do I do now?

I needed to get back inside my head. I needed to quiet the demons that were gathering in droves. I needed to see the sun set from the western side of the mountain.

So I drove up the winding road alongside Flagstaff Mountain after our pizza shenanigans at Abo's. I wasn't in the mood to converse much, even if Lily wanted to stroll down Pearl again. I needed to get my head right.

I leaned into the turns, left, right, left, right, tightening my abs like a workout. *Anything will help*. I drove with the windows down and head slightly out the window, sucking in the mountain pine air while the curls from my shaggy hair flowed behind me.

This was the reason to grow your hair out—to let it fly in the wind.

The farther up I got, the more crisp and cool the air was. Autumn had already descended in the mountains. Deep in the heart of Colorado the trees had already gone from green to yellow to red, and from the western slope of Flagstaff Mountain, I could catch a glimpse of the first snow on the tops of the fourteeners off in the distance.

The parking lot was nearly empty, as it was just minutes away from unofficially closing for the night. I parked and walked out among the trees to the rocky terrain on the west side of the mountain. It was a sea of tabletops and seats littered between towering trees that reached for the sky. From here, I could let my gaze scan the slopes to the west where the sun was beginning its descent from the sky. Soon the mountains would look like cardboard cutouts, navy blue silhouettes against a darkening sky. It was my favorite time of the day—when the sun set, illuminating their rocky ridges. From my backyard I could see the Flatirons, but from here, I could see Longs Peak to the north, with its pointed ridge touching the sky, which was washing over in a pink hue.

Sunlight pulled back from the landscape behind me, and soon the warmth went with it. I watched the orange ball in the sky fall at a gradual pace while the shadows came out between the trees, stretching into darkened corners.

I wondered how I got here, to this point, where finishing fifth at Liberty Bell was a bad race. At least in my head. A year ago I would've died to be in the mix, and now it was a letdown. A defeat.

When did the bar raise to such heights?

When I raised the bar in my head.

I could feel the landscape expectations shifting beneath my feet, and I wondered if I was the one leading the way. For a moment I yearned for the past when winning, or even placing in the top ten was a distant dream, not an expectation. Back when I could finish within the pack and the only one who really cared was me.

Now everything felt different. Everyone around me knew of my ambitions, and anytime I didn't reach my goals, I'd have to answer to that fact.

It was a double-edged sword, success.

Being anonymous among the crowd meant no expectations. Failure was only self-perceived. There was freedom with a low bar, because nothing really mattered.

But having goals and ambitions changed everything. It meant being decisive. Win or lose, it was all on your shoulders, on public display.

It meant being exposed.

Lily was right, if you can't deal with it, don't win the race.

No.

It's part of the pie.

If it was easy, anyone could or would do it. Chasing something lofty and difficult was worth it—but part of the difficulty would be the general public's view, their perception of it all. And that's something you don't realize until you start chasing big dreams. It's all the more reason to find the quiet, push out the outside voices, the ones that only nag or love when you're doing something big or small.

None of that matters.

All that matters is the pursuit. The journey. The adventure along the way. I could make the most of it or drown in the sea of opinionated voices, which included my own.

I closed my eyes the moment the sun set behind the mountains to the west and took a deep breath. Life was quiet in this moment, and because of that fact, I could hear myself think, hear myself breathe, hear myself *live*.

It's just one race.

Liberty Bell, just like State.

Just one race.

And you can change everything with just one race.

14

TEMPO

REDEMPTION.

"All right, everyone," Coach said with his hands high and wide, commanding the team like a captain about to lead us into battle. "This is the last tempo we have this season, so make it count. Remember your paces, and most of all—do *not* go out too fast. The goal above everything is to finish what's on your schedule."

I paced back and forth behind the team, unhurried, but anxious. I was eager to get the show on the road, eager to leave it all out there. Sure, it was just a tempo, but the finality of it all added gravity to it. It would be my last tempo of the season, and the year. I needed a confidence booster.

"All right, if you need to get one last drink, go ahead," Coach said. "And we'll get going here in two minutes. So do what you need to do now."

It was a calm afternoon with a gentle breeze that was already cooling my dried sweat. Little ripples stretched across the lake while the Flatirons loomed heavy in the distance. It was another bluebird day in Colorado, one of those fresh autumn days that lingers long into the evening.

The team hurried to the picnic bench to grab some fluids while I stood firm on the line now. I envisioned the start of the State meet. The colors. The sounds. The crunch of rocks beneath my feet. The tension. Grant Hemingway. My stomach leapt out from itself, and Coach could see I wasn't exactly *here*.

"Remember," he said," No faster than 5:30 the first four, then I want to see you blast the last two. See how fast you can go. Even if you hold 5:30s the last two, that's a great run."

I nodded.

"Last one, Baxter, so make it count," he said before tapping his watch and turning toward the team. "All right, everyone, let's get on the line!"

I shook my arms and hands out all the way down to my legs. Blake and Todd hovered beside me, while John and Chester lingered behind. I didn't look at this as any sort of race with them. It was a race against Grant Hemingway. It was a race against the rankings. It was a race against *myself*.

"Ready. . . and. . . GO!" Coach said with his stopwatch high. He punched the start button as he brought it down like a flag.

As eager as I was, I stuck to the plan.

I cruised through the opening mile at 5:31 with Blake, Todd, and Chester in my shadow. I felt easy, and somewhat contained. I broke the workout up into twos to make it easier in my head, and look at it more like a 5k. The first two miles were Mile 1, so you get out, but nothing crazy, sort of space out. Controlled. The second two miles were Mile 2, where you try to space out as much as possible without losing pace. Be mindful of the pace and everyone around, but don't do anything. The final two miles were Mile 3. Go time. Don't hold anything back.

I coasted through the opening two miles right in pace, 11:04 with the crew still intact. They let me take the pace, knowing I'd run on like a metronome. And Coach likely said, "No one should be in front of Baxter."

I scratched the itch a little the second two miles, inching up to 5:29, then 5:28. As I approached the four-mile marker in 22:01 with only Blake still chasing. I could see Coach nearly getting up on his toes in excitement.

"Here we go! Here we go! Two more miles, Baxter!" he screamed as I went by, jogging beside me. "Let's see what you've got!" Go! Go! Go!"

I felt a surge of blood pump through my body, like this was the bell lap. I could hear it echo across the field, somewhere deep inside my head. Tiny little goosebumps rose from my sweaty skin.

The Bell Lap.

I attacked the gradual downhill, letting gravity aid me in this quest. I was determined to put myself through as much pain as possible—that was what it would take to win a State title.

I pumped my arms and lifted my knees a little higher. There was no holding back anymore. I may die in mile six, but I'd at least give it a shot.

I was off into my own world now, and it was gradually getting more painful. The tiny slits in my eyelids shrunk and the pain escalated, but I didn't care.

As I climbed through the backside of the mile loop I thought of Penrose. The final two hills. Grant Hemingway. Getting fifth at Liberty Bell. The rankings. Anything to add fuel to my stride.

I could feel my jaw tightening from it all as I made my way back upwards toward Coach and the team, who were nearly all done now minus Blake, Todd, and Chester. I crested the hill and could see Coach there with his stopwatch and team hovering on both sides of the trails with water and Gatorade.

When a JV kid spotted me coming, he pointed and said, "Coach—there's Baxter!"

Coach looked up from his stopwatch in surprise, then back to his clipboard to quickly write something down.

"Come on, Baxter!" he screamed along with the team. "One more mile! Keep rolling! Keep rolling!"

I could feel the red line somewhere nearby now, though I still had some more gas in the tank. I pumped my arms a little harder as I cruised by the team.

"27:03 Baxter! That's a 5:02!"

I'm still hungry.

I bounded off my toes, feeling yet another surge of *something*. It wasn't where it normally came from. It was coming from *out there*. As if you get additional fuel reserves when there's redemption on the line, I don't know, but I still had a thirst for pain, even with a mile to go.

I replayed the previous mile, and it started to dawn on me that if I could crack five on this last mile, I might be able to break 32 minutes. I'd need a 4:56, which would be insane, but why not try? I wasn't even sure where that 5:02 came from—I wasn't thinking about pace, I was just focusing on the pain, and there was a lot of it now.

I leaned down the long gradual hill for the sixth time of the day, but this time there was no caution. I simply just tore down the hill as fast as I could. I could see the finish line now, figuratively at least. Last mile. Last mile. Last mile.

I focused one stride at a time, because anything beyond that made me feel more cautious, like I was spending the money in my bank too fast.

Don't be cautious now—rip it.

I crossed the wooden bridge that signaled halfway through the final mile, and knew that it was literally all uphill from here. But that didn't matter. None of it. I felt reckless and aggressive. I didn't care if I lived or died, I only cared about the pain. I gravitated toward it like a leech. It was the only way I knew I was alive, so I craved more of it. Living in the discomfort of the red line had somehow become *comfortable*.

Every stride was pain, but every stride had purpose. I no longer was afraid of the pain, or what would happen, because I had been living in it, and here I was. Still alive. Still running at five-minute pace.

Up and up the final hill, back toward reality, back toward the team and Coach and all the expectations I went. I thought of that final right turn into Penrose and heard the crowd cheering. I thought of the pain it'd take to get there without a shadow. I thought of hearing my father's trademark scream, "Come on, Baxter!" And my mother right next to him. I thought of crossing that finish line in first, finally. The relief, the weight lifting off the shoulders. I thought of all the smiles that would result.

I wanted that moment even more.

I gritted my teeth and kicked hard down the final stretch where the entire team begged me on. Coach stood on the side, stopwatch and clipboard in hand, screaming as his eyes widened when he saw the numbers click on.

"Come on, Baxter! All the way in! All the way in!"

I felt my shoulders tighten and my legs were strides away from hitting empty, but none of that mattered, because the pain was like candy, and I wanted more.

"32:02. . .32:03. . .32:04. . ." Coach read out as I cruised by the makeshift line.

I slowed to walk and put my hands up on my head, gasping for air. The pain gradually dimmed with each big breath. I circled back toward Coach who was shaking his head in disbelief.

"That was a five-minute last mile, Baxter."

"I was trying to break thirty-two," I said between gasps.

"I got you at 32:03," he said. "Baxter. That was an incredible run."

I paced back and forth still catching my breath, hands on my head, not yet absorbing what I just did.

"Get something to drink," Coach said, motioning to the picnic table where he had Gatorade waiting.

I nodded between gasps and turned to walk away, still searching for air. Still thinking about that final turn into Penrose.

15

HOMECOMING

I leaned on Lily's locker, waiting anxiously for her arrival. With all the chaos around the season, I hadn't really kept a watchful eye or ear out for Homecoming. It was a formality, and I really wasn't interested so much in going, though the thought of someone else taking Lily crawled under my skin and scratched.

I didn't like it.

So I had to do something about it.

I had rehearsed the scene in my head during History class. I'd be all awkward, per the usual, and say something along the lines of "If you're not busy Saturday night, do you want to go to Homecoming?"

And she'd be all taken aback, like, "Oh, okay, sure," with some hesitation, per the usual. She'd hide any real excitement, but she'd say yes, right?

The truth was I didn't know.

So here I was, leaning awkwardly on her locker, waiting. I dug my hands into my pockets to hide their sudden shakes. For whatever reason this was more stressful than any workout I'd done—I could control the variables while running, but this, Lily, was another beast. I never could figure her out, and so that's what made this so nerve-wracking.

Repeat after me: Would you like to go to Homecoming?

Why does Homecoming even exist? It's just another event created to make awkward guys like me feel all the more out, less confident. Then I'd have to go rent something nice to wear, or dig around in my dad's closet for clothes that are too big. I'd have to go buy flowers or a carnation or whatever it was I was supposed to give Lily. Then ask my parents for money so I could take her out somewhere nice to eat. And in Boulder, there's an abundance of nice places to eat, all over-priced. And not only would they be over-priced, they'd be packed. I'd have to call to get a reservation and hope that the rest of Flatirons High went somewhere else on this one night. But then again, Fairview and Boulder High are having their Homecoming dance the same Saturday, which meant every nice restaurant would be packed with teenagers dressed like adults, hormones raging, everyone with ulterior motives.

Maybe I should just take her to Taco Bell. Or Abo's.

And then there was the whole thing with the dance itself. I didn't even like to dance. What if Lily wanted to dance? *How do I even dance?* I didn't want to make myself look like an ass, but if I had to get on that dance floor and do anything beyond swaying side to side slowly then I'd clearly embarrass myself.

Okay, so avoid any and all dancing.

And where would we go afterwards? What if she didn't want to go home yet? What if she wanted to go up Flagstaff Mountain or NCAR like the couples do to go make out and wink wink? How would I even initiate that? How would I even decide when to end the night? If she wanted to stay out late then I wouldn't get enough sleep for Sunday's long run. I'd need an out, but I didn't want to be that lame, but if Lily Bissinger wanted any slice of me, I didn't think I'd deny her—no one would.

And then what? Were we dating? Were we a couple? Would that one night lead to many more like that? What if we went to different colleges? Would we stay together?

Homecoming seemed to offer too many questions, and so few answers.

Why even do this, again?

Oh right, so you wouldn't have to fret all night that she was dancing in the arms of another guy and would potentially go up on Flagstaff to lock lips with someone other than me.

I waited, and waited, and waited by her locker while all these questions rolled across my head in bright red letters like breaking news. I tried not to think about every last turn, but I was wired to play out the potentials, and the one I hadn't thought of once ended up being the one I should've thought of.

When Lily finally—finally—came around the corner, books tightly clutched to her chest, per the usual, she seemed surprised—I never really waited by her locker, so this was an uncommon sight.

"Baxter, what's up? Everything okay?" she asked, eyebrows raised and those big brown eyes beaming into me, per the usual.

"Yeah, yeah, I, uh, just had a quick question, no big

deal," I started, shifting my weight like I had on the starting line of the tempo run Tuesday.

She stared at me while I fumbled around to find my words.

Repeat after me: would you like to go to Homecoming?

"I, uh, just wanted to ask, uh, if you had, uh, anything going on Saturday night?"

"You mean Homecoming?" she asked.

"Yeah, uh, Homecoming, are you, uh, going?" My palms were sweaty but hidden in my pockets while I continued that nervous sway side to side. *Maybe I can dance?*

"Yeah."

Spit it out. Spit it out. Spit it out.

"Cool, cool, yeah, uh, so, I wanted to see if you, uh, wanted to go, uh, with me?"

Victory! Finally, I had put the words in my head onto paper, out into the world for her to finally hear. I felt the weight lifted off my shoulders, like winning County. I had finally done something that had gripped my mind. I could hear the music now, the balloons falling from the ceiling along with the confetti. Like a game show winner.

And then.

"Oh, yikes, Baxter." She let my name hang in the air, and I waited for her to catch it before I floated off and out the hall, somewhere else into the ether.

Her brown eyes went cold for a moment and I could sense the gravity shifting beneath my feet again. There was something I didn't know. *Stop the music. Retract the balloons and the confetti, we have an issue here.*

"I'm actually going with Todd," she said like an apology. "He asked Monday."

That little Shit.

"Oh, uh, oh, okay. Cool." I backpedaled. Or tried to at least. The one scenario I hadn't yet considered: she had already been asked and said yes. Here I was like some moron assuming she'd go with me, running through every possibility of the night, and the one thing, the one thing I hadn't played in my head was this one, right here. "That's cool, good. I, uh, cool. . . well, I uh, guess I'll go. See you later."

"Baxter," she said while I turned away. *Have I been here before?* "I am sorry."

16

ON THE ROAD

The best thing about not having a Homecoming date was that I had a great excuse not to go. No rental suit. No carnation. No having to embarrass myself on the dance floor. No awkward after-dance shenanigans. No nothing.

I could spend the night driving around in my Corsica, listening to music while I watched the sun dive behind the mountains like every other night. Only on this night, I'd be entirely alone in my car, lost in the music of whatever.

I had stared at the ceiling fan spinning in my room for hours after dinner, waiting for the clock to tick on past 8 p.m., when the dance started. That'd be my window of hitting the road. I guess a part of me was still a little embarrassed to not nab a date, and I really didn't want to be seen roaming around Boulder in my car, alone.

Surely, this hope was useless, because not everyone would head to the dance at the same time. To counter this, I had opted to head down 93 toward Golden. A sort of out-and-back drive. And there were plenty of places to stop along the way, trailheads I'd see most weekend mornings packed with Subarus and bikes.

At this time of the night they'd be vacant, and I could easily park and listen to music while scanning the details of the mountains to the west or the cityscape to the east.

Once you drive up and over the hill just to the south of El Dorado Canyon, the bubble ends. It's an odd spot where once you crest the hill you can see life on the other side of the vast open space—life *does* exist outside of Boulder. It's hard to remember this fact during the week when I never leave, but on the weekends it's a little easier to remember since we're almost always taking the big yellow bus up and over the hill to a meet somewhere in the Denver area.

But most days of the week life does not seem to exist outside the bubble, which makes driving up and over the hill all the more vital to one's sense of self; *remember how big the world is—it's bigger than the bubble.*

The world is bigger than signing a petition to keep Walmart outside city limits. It's bigger than the zoning of open space surrounding the city or the funding for the bike path heading northwest to Longmont. It's bigger than chia seeds and kombucha or the grand opening of a third running store in city limits. It's bigger than Blake and Todd's bickering, and Lily having a date for Homecoming and it not being me.

Running websites were an additional aid with all this "remember the world is bigger than the bubble" stuff—it forced me to realize that being good in town didn't exactly translate to being good in the state.

Back in the day you had to wait for your month

subscription of *Track & Field News* to see where you stood —and they didn't really cover high school. Now, all you needed was your phone.

You could conjure up this information on the bus ride back from the meet you just ran, or in the car while your parents are ordering Chick-fil-A. It's candy within reach.

You could hide from it all you wanted, you could avoid the rankings, the results, the stories and photos. But at the end of the day, you knew were you stood. And as daunting as that could be following a bad race, it was thrilling. It was truth.

And as much as I had come to hold a disdain for the rankings, I needed them. I needed to know where I stood, because in running it's not subjective, it's objective. Sure, during the cross country season there's some subjectivity to it, but ultimately the head-to-head matches don't lie— you can't hide from the truth on the course or the track.

That sort of objectiveness I came to love.

And in the objectiveness I could find a bigger world— I knew not only where I stood in Colorado, but in the country. It made everything relative, which if you had small dreams, simply washed them out like a quick 3 p.m. rain shower. But for someone with bigger ambitions, it was important to know the landscape through and through.

It was important to know what was on the other side of the hill.

Which, at this moment, was vastly changing.

The sun had already set over the rolling terrain of the foothills, but its rays had not yet receded over the four-teeners, which left a streak of light stretching across the Denver skyline. Glittering light sparkled on those downtown skyscrapers that were visible for nearly thirty miles on a clear day.

And clear days were a common thing along the Front Range. Well, mostly.

Most days you could see all the way down to Pikes Peak—a solid ninety miles to the south by Colorado Springs. Its year-round white cap contrasted against the vibrant blue sky and everything shaded gray below. You could trace your fingers along the mountains heading north, all the way up toward Longs Peak just outside Estes Park, and onward to the unknown territory of Wyoming.

Who goes to Wyoming?

The scope of the landscape was a lot like scanning the national rankings or results—you could see everything, and in doing so, feel so damn small.

A couple years back they integrated a ranking system that took your fastest mile and ranked it based on times against others in your state, and then beside that a national ranking. Whatever asshat who came up with this threw a wrench in a rainy April day for me the previous spring, when I realized I was 463rd fastest miler in the country.

463?

Dammit.

Coach's words echoed in my ears: *We've got work to do.*

But see, it's that precisely—knowing where you stand at all times of the day and night give you the opportunity to do something about it. It's the yardstick of the running world, constantly moving as the talent becomes more abundant.

It's that sort of information that made me wish I had

been born thirty years earlier, so I could've been in the top ten in the country.

Now everyone has access to this sort of information, meaning everyone has the opportunity to educate themselves, or play stupid.

You couldn't play stupid when you saw what I saw. It was counterproductive.

And from the parking lot beside 93 near the Rocky Flats, I could see that maybe it was a good thing Lily had a date to Homecoming, and that it wasn't me. I could stay off my feet, get to bed at a reasonable time, if I didn't stay up too late reading, and get some good sleep.

State was only four weeks away, and I'd need all the rest I could get if I was going to do something worth remembering.

17

FLATIRONS VISTA

THERE WAS A CHILL IN THE AIR THAT WOULD REMAIN throughout the run, which prompted me to really question if I should go shirtless. The temperature can be drastically different from the sun to the shade, and I had eighty-minutes on the schedule this morning.

Autumn had *finally* descended on the Front Range like a wave, washing all the trees in new colors. This meant colder mornings and lukewarm days. It was my favorite time of the year, because that scent of dried leaves that lingered in the air meant that State was just around the corner. *The Big Show.*

I tied my stale laces, dried from sweat of the summer, in the parking lot just outside of El Dorado Springs. I had an eighty-minute loop around Flatirons Vista with the most intimate views of the Flatirons. The route was a little challenging early on—the first thirty or so minutes were a gradual climb *into* the Flatirons. You couldn't really think of it as a whole, you had to break it up into sections. Then you cruised through the trees and between the god-like ridges of the mountains. Even from a distance the Flatirons look huge, but running on single track trails between them only enhances this fact. They look enormous.

Flatirons Vista had a bit of a locals-only-bro feel to it —most tourists didn't venture this far south of the bubble. It wasn't the kind of place you'd see huffing old women with fanny packs and white Keds, or men with straw hats and walking sticks they bought at REI. That was reserved for Mesa Trail or Green Mountain.

Even its own residents partook in its fruits occasionally.

You could explain this easily with the fact that the terrain wasn't for the faint of heart—you had to be somewhat of an endurance beast to handle these trails. Or a semi-professional runner. Or a highly trained high school athlete with an affinity for all things pain-related.

You get the idea.

The trail was unusually empty for a Sunday morning, or maybe I was just out there a little earlier than usual. I had created this habit of starting my Sunday long run insanely early, timing it to be finishing up when the Fairview High team was just getting started. This way they'd see me sprinting in, finishing my run before they were even breaking a sweat. In my own mind I figured anyone finishing up a run before 8 a.m. had to be a little crazy.

I played mind games with my competition.

Typically it'd be packed with cars with bike racks from some un-cleverly named post-collegiate running group. They always existed in shape-shifting forms in Boulder.

New team name, same runners, minus one or two, like rock bands.

There was Mother Love Bone, then without Andrew Wood, Temple of the Dog, with Chris Cornell and Eddie Vedder, then without Cornell, Pearl Jam.

But much of the same faces throughout the evolution of the group.

Yeah, post-collegiate running groups in Boulder were a lot like rock bands.

Typically I'd see one of the many of them in these parking lots on Sundays. They, and they as in all the various groups, always started around 7:30, though they tended to avoid each other. There was always a middleman who knew something about one group or another, so they'd vaguely communicate and make sure not to cross paths.

It was actually quite comical.

Clearly, there was some miscommunication, or a lost-in-translation about where each group would run today, because the parking lot was nearly empty.

I laughed a little at the thought of a few dozen runners seeking to *not* run with each other showing up at the tiny Boulder Res parking lot. They'd get out of their Subarus, avoiding eye contact, but frantically searching for *their* group. I thought the petty thing was a high school trait, but in Boulder it definitely oozed back out among the variety of post-collegiate groups who all had a better idea of how to train.

Inclusive in its exclusiveness.

Or was it the other way around?

I digress.

I didn't mind the quiet trails at Flatirons Vista,

because it meant that I could run along and listen to the quiet crunch beneath my feet echo out while I let my mind roam the rolling terrain and up the rocky ridges of the Flatirons.

No. I didn't mind this at all.

I ran up the long open dirt path while the terrain picked up on both sides of me. I could see my breath with each exhale—and I was glad to have kept a shirt on. I didn't really like running cold. I'd rather be slightly warm and get hot later. My fingers weren't saved from the crisp air, however.

Up and up the trail went, winding back and forth before entering the lone line of pine trees that stretched north and south along the ridge. This is where you leave the Front Range behind and enter *The Wilderness*.

Or so I told myself.

Baxter in the Wilderness.

I leaned into each tight turn like a mountain biker, taking the momentum into the next step. That gradual climb wasn't over yet, though it felt like it since I was running within the trees—I couldn't see the uphill nearly as much as I could when the trail was out in the open.

And then there's the break.

When the trees stop for a brief 200 meters to leave you out in the open vista—the Flatirons Vista—where you get an intimate one-on-one view of the second Flat-iron, which shreds upward like a guitar, exposed as true immortal rock, right in front of my very eyes. This was the reason I loved this route sooo much—this view right here.

I always felt small and insignificant in this one spot.

No. 9,999 in the rankings, in every event.

But there was something calming about this feeling. This feeling of microscopic existence. In feeling small, nothing mattered. Because life was too damn big to control every last step, so in feeling small, you could really just focus on each tiny step—that was the only way to really chew off the world without choking on the bite.

Baby steps—right?

You don't win a race by looking at all 3.1 miles as a whole, you break it up mile by mile, step by step.

Day by day.

Even then, creating a plan six months out to win State and looking at it on your calendar as a whole is overwhelming. Had Coach told me I'd nearly crack thirty-two minutes for a six-mile tempo back in June I would've laughed in his face and walked off, realizing that Coach was indeed crazy.

And here I was thinking I was the crazy one all this time.

Small bites. Baby steps. Whatever you want to call it, it works. And runs like the Flatirons Vista loop were a very physical, mental, and emotional reminder of this fact, because there was no bombing through this run. There were no sub-six minute averages—there were sub six miles on the way *down* back to the car, but the route itself had enough terrain changes, mostly climbs, that really took the air out of a fast overall run.

This too, I didn't mind.

Because this run wasn't about speed, it was about the view, *it was about the ride*.

And the ride was the most beautiful one in the Boulder area, another reason I didn't mind *not* sharing it on yet another Bluebird Day in Colorado.

I had this view, and these quiet trails, and these immortal rocks climbing out of the earth for air all to myself.

This right here was my church, my temple, my spiritual centering for the week.

Some people needed thoughts and prayers. Some needed to spew out their sins in tiny boxes into checkered windows. Some needed to be bound by a book so as to not rage on in a chaotic murdering spree.

Training wheels to becoming a better you. Floaties to keep you from drowning. Pre-packaged philosophies.

I didn't need all the bells and whistles. I got all my relief here on the quiet trails, the only audible noise my huffing and puffing mixed generously with the crunch of tiny pebbles and rocks that crumbled beneath my feet.

It really was that simple.

18

BREADCRUMBS

"How are you feeling?" Coach asked between breaths. It was another one of those few times we shared the final mile of the day's run barefoot on the grass. Coach and I circled the inside of the track solo while nearly everyone else had already packed up and headed inside, the day's task complete.

"A little tired, but okay."

I told a white lie. The reality was that my quads were a little sore from screaming down the hill at sub 6 pace on the way back to the car. I may have let some daydreams of State trickle to the front of my mind during Sunday's long run.

I told myself it was okay since I sat in the Boulder Creek for twenty minutes afterwards, letting my toes go numb. *Refreshing.* I watched a hobo wash his hair with shampoo on the other side of the creek and thought, *Well, at least he's washing his hair.* That's a far cry from the guys who actually take a piss in the creek. It's why my icing spot is so far up the creek—so as to decrease the chances of icing in piss-water.

The urine-infused waters were closer to the library, where the tourists flocked.

"Okay, well, let's make sure we get in some strides after this," Coach said. "And did you take it a little easier on yourself yesterday?"

"What do you mean?" I played coy.

"You know what I mean," he said with a laugh. "Eighty minutes and no more, right?"

"Right." I let the word linger in the air for a moment, not wanting to tell him it was eighty minutes at Flatirons Vista with the final two miles just under six-minute pace. *I couldn't help it.*

"Where did you run?" He pried for more. He knew my tricks. We had been doing this for over two years now.

"Flatirons Vista." I let the words dribble out like a question, knowing what he'd say in response.

"Ugh, Baxter." He raised his head and arms to the sky. The universal *Why?* "I said an *easy* eighty minutes. That's a tougher run. You know better."

"I know, I know." I began to plead my case. "It's just really nice out there."

"I know, Baxter, but you've got to listen to me." He began to plead his. "There is a plan. And it doesn't work if you don't stick to it."

"Well, I did do eighty minutes. That was part of the plan."

"Yes, you did, but eighty minutes at Flatirons Vista is more like ninety minutes everywhere else."

"So, ten minutes?"

"Baxter," he said, letting my name drop to a lower

tone. A dog that does a bad deed must be sent to the corner. "Come on. We're sooo close now. Let's be more cautious. I don't want you getting injured."

"I won't." I threw up the white flag. I knew he was right. I just get *overeager* sometimes. He's always had to throw a leash around me when I stray too far like an overly excited dog that just saw a few other dogs playing on a greener field across the highway. Otherwise I'd climb the ridge up and over toward Winter Park on our Rollinsville long runs then feel heavy for the next week. *But the mountain is right there.* Coach always knew when to snuff out my ambitions when they were destructive.

"Plus did you hear?" he asked. His tone went from pleading father figure to friend.

"Hear what?"

"About Grant Hemingway?"

"Oh, yeah! That Sean Roberson beat him?"

"He's beatable," Coach quipped. "I told you. If Sean can beat him, so can you."

We ran along the freshly cut grass in silence for a few strides while I absorbed this information for the second time in thirty-six hours. Sean Roberson beat Grant Hemingway by six seconds. I beat Sean by twenty-six seconds at County. *How does this equate?*

The Terminator was beatable. The kid who did 1,000 push-ups and sit-ups every night before going to bed. *I can't even do ten pull-ups.*

"And this is why I say you need to trust the plan," he said, lagging on each word one at a time to emphasize his point.

"Okay, okay, I get it, Coach," I said. "I will *try* to be more mindful."

We circled the track once more for the final lap before slowing to a walk. My feet were stained green and sore from Sunday's effort.

"All right, ready for a few strides?" Coach said, pointing back down the field. "Just four."

I turned and accelerated, hitting my top speed just after the fifty-yard marker, then slowed back down on the other end of the field. Despite the heavy feeling in my legs, I felt the pop off my toes with each stride. There was still some juice in the tank, even if I was little tired.

After slowing to a walk after my fourth and final stride, Coach came back over, clipboard in hand. "It's Monday. You know what that means."

"Still?" I grumbled.

"Yes, until you hit ten."

At the beginning of the season Coach prescribed me and only me some light weight lifting twice a week, and the cherry on top: pull-ups. Being weak and scrawny, I was only able to do four the first time. After that very low bar was set, Coach set the goal at ten before State.

"If you can do ten, you'll win State," he told me after a steamy August run in the gym. Ten at that time seemed like a 1,000. But in the coming weeks I had inched my way upwards toward the magical ten, hitting eight the past two times. But State was just weeks away, and I'd have to conjure up some magic to hit ten.

Like Coach said, "If you can do ten, you'll win State."

And if Sean Roberson can beat Grant Hemingway, and I can beat Sean Roberson, *I can win State.*

19

SWEEP IT UNDER THE RUG

"Baxter, wait up," Lily said, books clutched in their trademark position to her chest a few steps behind me.

"What?" I said, turning to give her a quick glance, but not slowing at the slightest.

"I said wait!" she said more sternly this time. "I need to talk to you."

I scurried through the crowd toward the double doors that led outside into the light, away from all the congestion and constipation of the inner walls of Flatirons High. I needed some air.

"Now?"

"Yes now."

You could say I'd been avoiding Lily since Homecoming. I guess I was pretty put off, not only by the fact that she had jumped at the chance for a date, but with One-Step Todd? *Really*?

When the sea of bodies cleared just before the door I used both hands to push open the heavy metal. In a flash of light everything turned from that florescent white to Colorado blue. The trees were already well on their way to color transformation, but the jagged rocks of the Flatirons always remained that grayish-brown-almost-beige-but-not-quite color.

"Baxter," she said, touching my arm to slow down my pace. "Please stop for one minute. I just want to talk."

I stopped finally, throwing up that figurative white flag, knowing that she'd chase me if I started to run. *Or maybe she wouldn't.*

"What? What's up?" I let the annoyance in my voice twang so she'd know I wasn't in her back pocket. *Such a power move.*

"Listen," she started, tucking the long brown curl behind her ear. I tried not to swoon. I needed to appear like I didn't care. Like I didn't need her and that she was wasting my precious time.

Such a drama king.

"I just wanted to apologize," she said, looking up at me with those big brown eyes. "For Homecoming."

"There's no need," I chirped, shifting my weight from side to side. Those brown eyes bore into me like they had every other time, and I did my best to divert. "I didn't ask you early enough, so it's fine."

"Well, it doesn't *feel* fine," she said. "You've barely talked to me since before. . ."

"It's fine." I tried to find my way through the maze of her prodding. "It's fine, it's fine."

I turned once again in escape, but she wasn't having it. Her soft hand that smelled like lilac touched my hand and I tried to not care without much success.

"Baxter," she pleaded. "Don't walk away. I want to talk."

"About what?" I said. "I already said it's fine. So we're good."

"You say that, but I don't believe you."

"Well, that sounds like a *you* problem."

I tried hard not to smile, or smirk, or give away any hint that I was enjoying this role reversal.

"Don't be like that," she said.

"Don't be like what?"

"An ass."

I exhaled. I knew there was no way around this. And I guess at the end of the day I didn't really want there to be. But I wasn't exactly the best when it came to being honest about my feelings.

My family had long ago perfected the whole sweep-it-under-the-rug existence when it came to real things, and it was one aspect I hadn't yet unlearned.

I pursed my lips and shrugged in that "What'll you do?" mime.

"Ugh," she said, throwing up her hands. "I don't get you, Baxter."

"Likewise," I chirped, wanting the argument because it meant attention, but really just wanting *her.*

"So, let's talk then." She reset. "I want us to be able to talk."

"Why?" I shot back. "Why do you want *us* to talk sooo much?"

"Because!" she said with those big brown eyes beaming on into new colors up the rage scale.

"Because what? That's not really an answer, you know."

"Because I *like* you!" she said, shaking her head.

Victory! I had gotten her to admit she liked me!

"You. . . what?" I hadn't really expected that response, though it was like music to my ears. Lily *liked* me? "I don't. . . I don't really understand."

"Ugh, you're such an ass," she said, slapping my arm with her history book. I pretended it didn't hurt, but it was a thick book. "What don't you understand about what I just said?"

"I don't know, you just—you went to Homecoming with Todd."

"Baxter, he asked me first." She remained locked in on me with that A+ eye contact while I searched the pavement for words.

"I know, I know, but *come on*, it's One-Step Todd."

"I knew that bothered you!"

"Of course it did."

"And why is that?"

Role reversal.

I frantically searched for a non-incriminating response somewhere in the thin air around us or in the pavement beneath my feet but came up with nothing. I sensed that commonly known word vomit of "Things you may regret" climbing its way up my throat or out of my head, wherever that stuff comes from. I didn't have any plastic cup to spew into, only out into the ether, which happened to share an ear with Lily.

"Oh, come on, Lily," I diverted. "You know why."

"No, I don't," she said, clearly playing the Baxter-card of stupid now. She smirked, knowing that she had me in her back pocket, and I tried for the umpteenth time not to swoon. I hated her and loved her at the same time for being her. "I need you to say it."

"Say what?"

"Tell me why going to Homecoming with Todd bothered you."

"One-Step Todd," I corrected.

"Whatever. One-Step Todd."

She stood with her hands on her hips now, the real power pose. If she didn't break me here she never would. But Lily didn't lose. She was a winner. And she knew how to break people down, including me.

Against my better judgment, or perhaps against my long-held tradition of remaining truly closed off to those around me, the words began to trickle up my throat in staccato bursts that I couldn't swallow back down.

Dammit.

Cue Lily removing the rug from under my feet in three. . .two. . .one. . .

"Because. . . I. . . I like *you*," I responded.

Lily cracked a mischievous smile, exposing those blinding white teeth, compliments of her dentist father. Then she wrapped her tiny arms around my frail body and squeezed until I couldn't breathe.

We're we dating now?

It was one of those weird moments where I had clearly been out-dueled, but it wasn't necessarily a bad thing.

Can you still claim victory in a loss?

20

ONE STEP FORWARD, TWO
STEPS BACK

OVER THE NEXT WEEK I CAME TO THE DEPRESSING realization that no, Lily and I were in fact not dating. It was some sort of formality with her, I don't know, that she had to make things "right" with us, and be honest that she "liked" me, but clearly our definitions of "like" were entirely different.

Just as before, she continued to baffle me with her antics. She wanted me to know that she liked me, but not enough to date? Something like that. It clearly made sense to her, but I was the complete idiot who wasn't understanding her Latin.

This awful realization came into play when after Saturday night's Abo's dinner, she opted to stay out rather than go for a drive with me. I figured if she liked me, she'd come with. But nope. I was wrong.

This made for a few hours punching the keys on my cell phone in a text fight. I never help myself when it comes to these things. I always make them worse by wearing my heart on my sleeve.

"You don't have to be *so dramatic*," she said in one text, which promptly led to me turning off my phone before hurling it across my room in an angry fit of wounded pride.

We had just taken a step forward only to take two back.

I let out some of this excess anger on my run with Blake, who seemed to be the only one willing to hammer down to six-minute pace along the Creek Path, or perhaps the only one willing to listen to me brood.

We swayed down the gradual downhill with the bikes that whirled by us, those mechanical butterflies of nostalgia.

"She just makes—no damn sense," I spit out unedited in staccato bursts while not slowing the pace one bit.

"Dude—she is—a little—different," Blake responded in an exhale. "I'm not—trying—to be mean—just—I wouldn't—want—to date her."

"Thanks, Blake—that's really—helpful."

"I'm—just saying," he continued. "She's—difficult."

"I know—right?"

"Oh—yeah."

"I'll—never—understand—her."

"Maybe—you don't—want to."

We ran along in silence for a minute. My chest was beginning to burn from the effort of having a real conversation while hammering down the Creek Path, passing the hobos in ripped flannel. Or maybe they weren't homeless, just rich adults in overpriced clothing. In Boulder you never really can tell.

"What do—you mean?" I finally pushed out. I was at

a crossroads. I wanted to be with her, but I also didn't. She had a power over me I didn't like admitting.

"Dude—she's a—high school—chick."

"Yeah—and?"

"In a—year—you'll be—in college."

"So?"

"Dude."

"What, Blake?"

"Can we—slow down?"

We had already clipped off four miles hovering just over six-minute pace, though it was mostly downhill. I hadn't realized how much Lily was fueling my stride.

It's always something.

We pulled the pace back to a more reasonable clip, but still a few turns ahead of Todd and Chester.

"I'm just saying," Blake started again with a chest half-full of air now. "Like, if she's gonna be difficult, don't bother."

He had a point.

"I know. But maybe I want to bother, you know?"

"Well, then you're wasting your time—you've got to get *your* crouton, remember?"

"What do you mean?"

"Grant Hemingway. Didn't you hear?"

"That he ran a crazy 15:07 course record at Pat Amato? Yes."

"*That* is why you shouldn't be wasting your time chasing girls. You've got a State title to win. You can't be wasting effort that'll take you away from *that*. You can bet that Grant Hemingway isn't chasing girls who are wasting his time. This is your last shot to do this, so do it. Lily will be around afterwards, but once the race is over, it's over."

Dammit, Blake.

"But what if I want to share the night following that State title with someone. Say, Lily?"

"Geez, Baxter," he laughed. "You're so full of shit."

"Yeah, she's said that much once or twice before too."

"No, but I mean it in a different way," he said. "Like, you sort of gravitate toward that challenge."

"What the hell does that mean?"

"I don't know. You like it?"

After a few strides in silence, I needed to hear more. I needed to know what it seemed everyone else knew about me that I didn't know about myself.

"Elaborate, please."

"Well, Baxter." Blake turned into teacher. I swear, this guy was destined to be a teacher or a coach one day. He had this explaining voice that was all matter-of-fact. "If Lily was easy, you wouldn't want to be with her."

"Define easy." I played his game.

"Well, not easy the way I view easy, but easy as in she makes you work for her attention, you know?"

"Continue."

"Like, you like her because of that fact. She's playing games with you, and you're letting her, and as much as you bitch about it, you enjoy it somehow."

"Oh, come on."

"No, hear me out, man. It's like running."

"What?"

"Like running. If you were the best and could beat everyone without a real effort, would you really care? Would it be worth it?"

Good point.

I hated admitting that Blake was right, only because

he was one of those guys that relished those moments—he was the "I told you so" guy, but he was right.

When we hit Arapahoe we turned south back toward Flatirons High with the sun inching its way toward the tips of the mountains to the west. I bit my tongue the whole way back, fighting the urge to give Blake his due. It was pride versus pride, but he was a few steps ahead of me on this topic, and I had to give it to him.

"Dammit, Blake," I said. "When did you get all wise?"

He shrugged with a giant pixie grin, hands up. "I do what I do. It's what I'm really gooder at."

"Did you just say gooder?"

"Dammit, Baxter."

21

THE PASSENGER

"Remember the plan." Coach eyed me hard as if I'd deviate from The Plan for some rebellious reason.

I was double-knotting the thin laces on my white Zoom Victory's. They were a bit stale from their last outing, which included a creek crossing and a ton of sweat.

"Got it," I said, releasing him from his parenting duties.

"And just remember, stay loose out there, it's just you. Feel it out, roll when you want to, but nothing before the halfway point, okay?"

"Got it."

I was typically short in these pre-race moments. I didn't like conversation much as it was, and this wasn't *really* a race. It was a dual meet with Longmont, and I usually wouldn't be racing on a Thursday afternoon in such a mundane meet, but Coach wanted me to spike up as a workout.

"Race on tired legs," as he so adequately put it.

Sure thing.

I suspected an additional purpose behind spiking up for a mid-week race: an ego-booster, since there wasn't really any competition outside Blake, or Todd, or Chester, and I'll admit, I had taken a shot to my pride with getting my ass handed to me at Liberty Bell, and then hearing about Grant Hemingway's mortality, then his huge run at Pat Amato, and all that Lily drama, my mind wasn't exactly in the most confident of places.

Autumn lingered in the air, swirling colorful leaves up into the afternoon chill. The trees danced with the wind, and I found myself mesmerized by their beautiful white noise for a moment. My mind went backwards in time, backwards to those days on the soccer fields at Fort Carson when my dad would coach our team, back when the sun would pull its rays back across the mountains, leaving us in the shadows on the field below. This would signal my dad to talk with another dad who coached another team to set up a scrimmage to end the day on a light, more fun note. Soon we'd be playing in the dark, only able to see the white stripes of the ball roll across the neatly cut grass and the white goal posts. My stomach would rumble in hunger, and soon I'd be home in front of a warm bowl of homemade spaghetti that my mom made. Her recipe was some sort of secret, or it felt that way at least. After that I'd shower, running hot water over my tired muscles, my stomach now full and my body tired and ready to sleep —

"Baxter, let's go!" Coach said, snapping me from my trance.

I trotted over the starting line where just over two dozen others stood in only two sets of singlets. The lack of color oozed dual-meet. It was almost strange *not* to see every color on the starting line.

My quads remained in their perpetual state of fatigue from all those half-mile hill repeats, and my calves were still loosening up. I had gotten used to this body-coma the past few weeks on the hope of Coach's Plan.

"It'll pass," he'd say. "Trust the plan."

After a summer of eighty-mile weeks, you learn to function when always tired, although this was a new kind of tired. It included more soreness. Either way, Coach had taken me from fifty-fourth at State my sophomore year to fourth my junior year. I trusted he knew what he was doing.

The one thing missing from this race was anxiety—I had none. I stood up patiently on the starting line while the starter raised his gun. I knew I wouldn't have to battle much for space and that I could run a five-minute clip off the starting line, and not the usual suicide thirty-second 200 to get out front. I realized how much stress boils when you have 200 competitors on each side of you. Here I only had about twenty-eight.

I breathed a little easier, stood a little looser, and my mind actually had the space to look at this for what it was: *a race and nothing more.*

It was a bit underwhelming when the gun shot and just over two dozen of us ran off into the field. I neglect to use the word "storm" with such little numbers because it was almost anti-climactic, like the start of a tempo run, only instead of trainers we had colorful spikes.

It was an out-of-town preview.

But there was business to take care of, even if it was.

Nearly everyone on our team had been given their

own set of orders, a *Plan* to follow, so no one went out with me at just over five-minute pace.

Coach's instructions were simple: 5:05-5:10 pace through two miles, then *whatever*.

Within the first mile I was already out, running along the grassy path without a shadow. My mind wandered off to the shady trails that climbed between the trees and up Green Mountain. Back to the quiet of when all you can hear is your own heavy breathing and the sound of your feet gliding along the trail like musical notes in a flurry of a song.

5:04. . .5:05. . .5:06. . .

It was the most mundane of mile-marker splits. Perhaps because it was a race, but a workout, but even a workout felt like it held more gravity. This being dressed up as a race felt more informal than anything else.

It was just another stroll in the park.

I cruised along the path, which went from thick grass to pounded-down dirt along the creek, passing a few colored shirts of parents or coaches or JV runners, standing by the sidelines.

The path did a tight U-turn over a cement bridge before turning back on the other side of the creek. At this turn I glanced slightly to see that Blake, Todd, and Chester were running according to plan as well, in a tight pack shielding John—the goal was to pull him along to a PR.

I felt like a locomotive, steaming along the flat land-scape to some distant Western town. Everything burned, but nothing mattered. I was tired but didn't care. In all reality, I wasn't even thinking about it.

I was daydreaming.

Off somewhere between the pines, dancing along the rocks up and up Green Mountain. Stopping for a quick gaze west at the snowy peaks where winter was already descending. I thought of clocks and that inevitable tick that never slows or stops. Time, always moving forward, and so must I.

I only woke from my reverie at the sight of Coach standing by the two-mile marker, clutching the stopwatch with his right hand while his left held the clipboard, ready to make notes.

10:08. . .10:09. . .10:10. . .

"All right, let's get it, Baxter!" he said, dropping the stopwatch and clipboard for a moment to curl his hands around his mouth in a makeshift microphone.

I thought back to that tempo and how his words sounded nearly identical.

Not so much anxious as excited.

I made a purposeful decision to lean forward and pump my arms a little more, a caffeine-to-the-bloodstream move, as if I was attacking a field of tiny grass blades beneath my feet.

My only competition was myself.

Despite the physical gesture, my mind remained detached from my body. I was running in automatic, phoning it in, *but not?*

I wasn't thinking about place or time, I wasn't even thinking about Grant Hemingway or State or Lily. To paraphrase the great Forrest Gump: *I was just running.*

My mind shifted like gravity beneath my feet to the very stride and step I was on. Not the next one, or the one after that, but the very moment I was in. It was like looking at life through a microscope. Everything was simplified to its singular being.

Not one. Two. Three.

But one. One. One.

Somewhere in the last mile I shed everything. Even the sweat dripping off my elbows flicked up and *onward*. I felt the cool breeze across my forehead. My long shaggy hair drifted behind me, and I felt in sync with the world around me. I was turning at the same rate the earth rotated. There was a connection that went beyond mind and body. It just *was*.

I, like everyone on the sides of the course, was looking on, but from within. Like a tiny speck inside my mind watching movements through the tiny slits of my eyelids. I couldn't feel anything, because I was a spectator too, but a passenger most of all. A passenger on this locomotive that was indeed steaming across the terrain, somewhere, *on*.

There was no before or after, or the stride I was in. And as I looped back around the soccer fields toward the finish, I remained oblivious to my surroundings, which had drastically changed upon my return to the world near the parking lot.

Curious onlookers hovered by the finish line as I cruised down the final straightaway, not even a sprint, just a hard run on in, still somewhere in my reverie of time and space.

15:18. . .15:19. . .15:20. . .

When I came to a stop I hadn't even processed the time, or the gasps that seemed to be hovering on all sides of me. From the inside out, it was an emotionless moment, it simply *was*.

Like the entire race itself, it was an anti-climactic affair, and when it was all over I simply walked back to the team tent to get something to drink, sweat dripping to the ground now. Within a minute I had returned from wherever it was I went.

After the dust had settled and the aching muscles returned on the bus ride back to the school hours later, it was like looking at a painting I had done, only I couldn't remember ever holding the brush. It was unfamiliar, as if someone else had done it, and I was just a passenger in the vessel. *Someone else was driving.*

"That was a 5k, right?" I asked Coach, who was just as shocked as I was.

"Yeah, I measured it three times."

"Are you sure?"

"Yes, Baxter."

22

THE PLACE BEYOND THE MOUNTAINS

IN THE DAYS FOLLOWING THE DUAL MEET I KEPT recalling the race, trying to understand where I went, or what happened. It was like a complicated math equation I somehow figured out after bumping my head but couldn't explain how I got there.

A math teacher's nightmare student.

Now, I can play the piano like a master!

Coach had continuously asked me how I felt during the race, and when I knew I was running that fast, particularly in that last mile, but I never really had an answer. It just *was*.

He, like any good coach, wanted to figure out how to duplicate the result. Likewise, I was baffled by the experience, and trying to do the same thing. How do I get back to *that* place?

The place beyond the mountains, as Coach so aptly put it, where time stopped and all that mattered was the exact singular moment I was in. Life seemed simple then —how do I return to that?

It was as if I had a near-death experience, and Coach wanted to know what I saw on the other side. He prodded me with questions. Any information could help create a playbook on how to get back to that place.

"Were your legs still feeling heavy in that last mile?"

"Did you eat or drink anything different beforehand?"

"Did you do all of Sunday's long run?"

"Where did you do Sunday's long run?"

"How many strides did you do the day before?"

"Did you get in your morning run?"

We trotted along the dirt road just beyond the Boulder Reservoir while he went on taking mental notes of my answers. Coach wanted to make sure I stuck to the Plan in those final weeks, so he opted to run step for step with me during my long run. The dirt had been packed from a midnight rainfall, proof that soon it'd be winter. Though I didn't mind—typically the dirt was loose and would dust up every time a Subaru with mountain bikes propped on top went whizzing by.

I was being quizzed with rapid-fire questions, though I didn't exactly have the answers.

The reality was I really didn't know what was different. It was just one of those moments that sort of happened.

When thinking goes out the window and stuff just happens.

That's the reality that I was having trouble explaining to Coach. I was just following the cues, and on the course, that was the plan—to push the final mile as fast as I could go. Now, neither of us thought I'd drop a 4:45. That's where things get a little foggy.

"I don't really know what happened." I finally gave in

to my own disbelief. "I mean, are you still sure that course was accurate?"

"Yes, Baxter, it was accurate."

He sounded annoyed by my question, and with good reason—I had asked it a few dozen times already. "Well, tell me what you felt like during that last mile, and we'll go from there."

"It was weird, really." I tried to find the words. "I was entirely present in the moment, and not like other races. This was different. It was like I was *transcending the bullsh—*"

"Don't say that word."

I used my mock southern preacher voice, but the joke was lost in Coach's ears. He was never a fan of cuss words, so we used them sparingly around him, if at all. He was okay with all the teenage-boy banter, but when it came to cuss words or degrading ideas, he made it known that it wasn't okay. That sort of language was reserved for when the adults left the room.

"Okay, okay, I just mean, I felt like I was rising above, or detaching from, myself. Like an out-of-body experience, and some little minion was running the controls inside me, like *Men In Black*, you know?"

"So, you're telling me you felt like you had a little alien controlling you from the inside, while you just sat and enjoyed the ride?"

"Yeah, that's pretty much it."

"Well, do you think we can get in touch with this little guy and ask him to do it again?"

"I'll see what I can do. He's on a pretty tight schedule."

We took the single-track trail off the dirt road on the

northwest side of the res to loop around, and to get off the road that was rapidly turning into a highway. Sundays out by the res always brought a slew of cars and noise, which made holding a conversation about as easy as a live concert. Destined for headaches in the morning from all that loud screaming of a conversation.

I'll admit to being a little over-dramatic, but you get the idea.

The single-track trail on the north side of the res was much more quiet and calm, and it ran alongside the aqueduct for a bit, which meant the only other bodies on the trail would be people walking their dogs.

"So, tell me about this little alien controlling you from the inside. Does he control what you say too?"

"Sometimes"

"Well, that makes more sense."

"Aw, come on, I was joking!"

"So am I!" Coach sucker punched my arm mid-stride and let out a laugh. "But more seriously, was it that, detached?"

"What?"

"What you felt, you said you felt like it was an out-of-body experience."

"Yeah, something like that, or what do you call it again? The Place Beyond —"

"The mountains, the place beyond the mountains."

"What does that even mean? The place beyond the mountains? It sounds like a secret shack where a murderer takes his prey, like a Stephen King horror novel or something."

"Definitely not quite so gory," he said with a laugh.

"The phrase sort of came to me when I was talking to my dad once before he died."

We ran on in an awkward silence for a bit. I remember the story about Coach's dad dying from cancer, but he spoke of it sparingly. I could sense he was still working through the details of it all, but he was somewhat in awe of the experience. There was a sort of respect for the whole ordeal, like he wasn't mad about it, he *understood*. Understood that death was a part of life, and it was something his father clearly instilled in him. But my family, with its knack for sweeping things under the rug, feelings and sympathy among them, I didn't feel like I had the tools to really go down that road and understand what Coach talked about sometimes, so I let him find his words.

"Once we were talking about what was coming," he continued. "He mentioned that there was a place beyond the mountains between this world and the next, and it was where great athletes and artists and innovators go in their more prominent moments. He had this theory that all great things in life come from this place, and was neither alive nor dead, not on earth or heaven. It was somewhere in between, beyond definition, beyond our understanding. And everything you've said about the experience sounds like *that*."

I loved Coach in these moments, when he'd get philosophical about things. He challenged me to define what I felt or what I saw. He challenged my way of thinking about life and death, and it inadvertently shaped my own philosophies, which were rapidly evolving. And he always spoke with hints of question rather than answers. There was never a wrong or a right, just an *is*. Everything was open to interpretation, and he said as much.

"We might see or hear the same thing, but our past experiences change the way we perceive and understand it," he once told me while we climbed up the long gradual hill toward the pavement on Magnolia before throwing a curveball on what was an otherwise serious conversation. "And right now I perceive this hill to be the end of my energy on this run, I'm *exhausted!*"

23

TENSION

WHAT ONCE WAS AN ENJOYABLE EXPERIENCE HAD become tense in the weeks following the dual. Dinner, well, second dinner, had become an anxiety-filled bowl of questions and answers, and I guess you could partially blame me for that.

I had become consumed with *The Task*, winning State, and it had clearly taken a bit of a toll on those around me, particularly my parents.

My father would bombard me with questions the moment he had cleared his plate. This made the clatter between scoops of mashed potatoes or slicing of steak a little uneasy for my mom, who tended to avoid the topic all together.

This left the driving of the conversation to me or my father.

"So there's a chance?" My father asked, wiping his mouth clean with his used napkin, a dicey move given that it was the same napkin he placed his jalapeño on.

Once, after washing the dishes clean from dinner when I was eight I mistakenly touched the mostly eaten jalapeño before picking my nose. Within the hour my nose was burning from the act, and I spent the majority of the night running cold water over my face. Little did I know that this would only make it worse.

I haven't touched a jalapeño with my bare hands since.

"Yeah, if the rankings were right, and they're not, then I should be in the mix," I said between bites.

"Don't talk while you're eating."

"Sorry."

"And you're still talking."

"Sorry."

That look of disappointment: I'd seen it many times before. My father was like the Flatirons, looming high in judgement, always watching.

"Well, mijo, who else is there to beat?" he continued on, after allowing me to clear my throat.

"Grant Hemingway, of course."

"That's the kid that won the stage races, correct?"

"Yeah."

"Yes," he corrected me.

"Yes."

"Anyone else? Or is it just him?"

I was once again being quizzed, this time on the competition. But when my father asks a question, you answer.

"There are a few others. The Niwot kid, Sean Roberson. And uh. . . I think the Fairview kid, Ryley Ohlson, could be good too. He always shows up at the end."

"Is that the kid who barely trains in the summer?"

"Yeah, but he's super-talented."

"Yes."

"Yes."

"Imagine if he trained year-round." He let out a low whistle.

"I'm glad he doesn't," I joked.

"Well, son, we should call your sister and see if she's available that weekend," he said, moving from the table to the kitchen to clear his plate. "She might want to be there."

"Unless it doesn't go well," my mom chimed in.

Ouch.

"Thanks, Mom."

"I didn't mean it like that, I —"

"Jesus, Evelyn. We're trying to stay positive here, and you're talking our son down."

"I said that wasn't what I meant, Scott!"

She stood up from the table, plate in hand, prepared to multi-task and battle with my father while finishing off the dishes.

He was heading back to Baghdad in a few weeks, and because of this fact the tension had really grown between the two of them. Every little conversation was heavy. It was like walking on ice between the two of them. Always. You never knew who'd blow up first, and for what reason.

I quietly ate the remainder of the thin steaks and mashed potatoes while my parents rolled into another one of their nightly arguments that either pertained to my sister's college tuition or my inability to do the dishes. I always slacked so they wouldn't ask me to do them, but that rarely worked.

I had grown accustomed to muting them out when

they argued. It was always something. So I went back into my cocoon, that safe little orb that circled me when I would think of State. How the race would play out. The surges. The colors. The noises. Soon they were just a gentle hum in the background while I doused my steak with more A1 sauce, something my father said would ruin it, but not for me.

I retreated into myself. The only safe spot that existed.

In my head, or on the course, everything made sense. Beyond that, I had no idea. Lily was always confusing, and my parents always had their bickering. People in general were a mystery to me, and on nights like this, I had no real impulse to figure anyone out.

Every time my parents argued it always seemed like it was really something else they were arguing about.

This time the surface argument was my mother's negative comment that I might not want my sister around if I bombed at State. But there was always something else. *Always.*

When they took their argument off into the living room I quickly washed my plate and darted for the door.

My mother always had this habit of cleaning while arguing with my father. She'd stack magazines on the table into a neat pile or pick up pillows and place them in the corners of the couch. She needed to do something with her hands, while my father would stand firm in one place, hand on hips like a statue.

It was almost comical. Almost.

But I needed to get out. I needed some fresh air, something to wash away the tension of what was going on inside the house and that comment.

I needed to move around, let my body and mind roam under the starry night sky. Where everything was open.

24

SECOND CHANCES

"Mr. Reeves, will you stay for a moment?"

Blood rushed through my body, and I went from a solid 98.6 degrees to a fever. I wasn't sure if I did something wrong, but Mrs. Blake's voice indicated concern.

"Sure, Mrs. Blake." I tried not to let my voice quiver in a mixture of anxiousness and excitement.

Mrs. Blake wanted to see me *after class*?

Everywhere around me there was motion as the class was quickly gathering their things and heading onward, to the hall, into the sea of colors and noise. This wash of white noise was quickly erased once it was just me and Mrs. Blake, who sat quietly behind her vast wooden desk.

It made her look even more petite. Her eyes scanned something in front of her.

I waited. And waited. And waited.

Eventually her curious eyes rose up from whatever it was in front of her and onto me. She zeroed in on her prey from the other side of all those papers and books and notebooks. I was the deer in headlights.

"Baxter," she started. Oh, my knees went weak just having her attention. "We have a bit of a problem."

Cue the sirens. This was *not* good.

"A problem?" I uttered in such a mixed moment.

"Yes," she said. "See, you're not doing so hot in my class."

She let the fact linger in the air for additional tension.

"I'm not?"

"No, you're not, but you know that already."

I do?

"And see, the problem I have with this is that there's no reason for you to be doing this bad."

"It's that bad?" My mind raced around the room, not exactly overly concerned with my grade but nervous at having Mrs. Blake's undivided attention.

"Well, the truth is, it should be *a lot* better," she said. "Baxter, I can tell when you're not here."

"I'm always here, though."

She had the power to make you question even the basic of truths just by batting her eyelashes and smiling.

"In terms of physical attendance, yes, that's correct, but that's not what I'm talking about."

Okay?

"I'm talking about mentally being here, in your seat, in my class, paying attention, *that's* what I'm talking about."

Yikes.

She had me there. I typically spaced out during her class and daydreamed about the coming workout or race. Sometimes I even just imagined us running away to some beach, perhaps Key West, and we could visit the Hemingway House and talk literature and make sand castles. Then we could watch the sun rise from the beach in the morning before I went for a run, and do the same in the evening while we talked about our day and what we wanted to do with life.

I was sure her husband wouldn't mind.

"Okay."

I wasn't really sure how to remedy this situation. She was right.

"And the reason this is a problem is because I know you're better than this. You know you're better than this."

I do?

"And don't give me that disbelief BS, I know you know what you're doing. You just get bored." She stood up from her desk and walked around it, eyeing the paper in her hand before sitting on the front of her desk right in front of me. Her brown eyes read into me and I imagined that was how she got everyone. "And I get it. I get why you're bored. The truth is I have to teach this stuff." She signaled the mysterious paper in her hand. "Every teacher has to stick to the syllabus. And the truth is it's boring. I get it."

I sat motionless, afraid to make eye contact or I'd melt away in this wooden chair and down onto the floor. Then she'd have to clean up the mess of me.

"Okay," I whispered, nodding along with her in our most brilliant of moments together. "So, what's—uh, next?" I spit out.

"I'm glad you asked," she said, revving that engine like we all do on the starting line while the starter raises the gun in the air to send us off into a painful quarter of an hour. "Here's what I propose."

Oh, so soon? Yes. My answer is yes. Definitely yes.

She moved around the desk, back to her chair, her throne, paper in hand and still casting glances at me while she moved.

"You're going to write me a paper."

"A paper?"

"Yes, a paper. To prove that you know this stuff." She waved the paper in her hand again. "Prove that you know how to do this by writing me a paper."

"A paper—on what?"

"It can be anything. Anything you want."

"Anything?"

"Baxter, I know you can write, and this is your chance to prove that you understand what you're doing. That you're not one of those kids who can't read music but can *really* play."

Words trickled though my head, but I couldn't catch them fast enough to actually have a real conversation with Mrs. Blake. She was too fast.

"Or how about," she said and stared off into space for a brief moment as if an idea was drifting through the air and she was about to grab it with her hands. "Write about your last race."

"My last race? What?"

"Your last race. The meet record."

"You heard about that?"

"Yes, Baxter, your English teacher reads the newspaper." She shook her head and smiled.

"So you want me to write about the race? Like, what part?" I pried for more direction. This sounded too good to be true. A race with no competitors, *sort of.*

"How about you write about the race from your perspective. I want to read *your* perspective of how it went. Bring me along with you. Take me into your world."

Yes, Mrs. Blake.

My heart fluttered at hearing those words coming from her soft red lips, even if I knew I wasn't translating it correctly.

"So do we have a deal?"

"Yes, Mrs. Blake."

25

MUSINGS

I SAT UNDER THE DIM LIGHT BY MY DESK WHILE MY tired eyes scrolled down the bright white screen, waiting for a flush of energy to rush through my body. I clicked from left to right, then down on the new rankings. After the whole dual meet, word got out, and I knew that this would likely thrust me into the position of having a bullseye on my back heading into Regionals.

The world had gone to sleep around me, but I wasn't ready to call it a night just yet. I had a half-eaten bag of purple Skittles and a fresh blue Gatorade waiting to be devoured. I wanted to savor this moment. One that I was sure I'd get my due.

I scrolled over the big bold letters of 5A Boys Rankings, and clicked, knowing that on the other side of this door would be what I was searching for. The internet lagged on this busy Boulder night, and the anticipation was killing me.

When the screen finally revealed itself, my heart dropped.

Number 3.

Are you kidding me?

What the hell is it going to take to get ranked higher?

I fumed around my room, circling the tiny highway from my bed to my desk to the heap of clean clothes that lay in a pile by the wall.

I was sure the dual meet would've made me legit in the eyes of everyone else in the state, but third? *Really?*

Is that what they all really think?

I slammed the laptop closed and made my way for the door. I needed to walk. I needed air. Sure, they're just rankings, but I hated being underestimated, or that's at least how I saw it.

Doubted.

I slid my arms into my navy blue team jacked, zipped it up to the neck, and hit the street.

The streetlights created circles of light that I walked between, hovering in the darkness where no one could see. I walked a little slower in the dark and faster through the light. I always had a sense of another set of eyes on me, and I didn't want anyone seeing me brooding down the street.

You look like a real creeper when you're walking around alone, which is why I typically waited until the sun had taken back all its light so I could walk under the cover of darkness.

An invisibility cloak of sorts.

My mind raced.

What else did I need to do to be taken seriously? I knew rankings were just rankings—they didn't decide the winner of the race, but come on.

And then there was Dad. He was leaving in two days.

Started packing days ago. After his month home he was always chipper when packing to go back, like he couldn't wait to leave. As if life here was so boring.

I never could understand him.

Senior year. I was trying to win a State title, dammit, and he was counting the minutes until he got to board a plane and head back across the world.

If I won and he wasn't there, what the hell? What was the point in that?

And just right there, in this moment between the lights, I had to ask myself, was I doing this, chasing this dream, for me? Or for him? *For his affections?*

I didn't like the questions I was asking myself. But here I was, pissed at the latest rankings and pissed that my father seemed more excited to leave than to be here with his family.

"I can't be just a husband or just a father," he once told me while tears dripped out of my eyes when he took this job. Just?

Just?

And in that moment I grew a new distaste for the word "just."

It implied a less-than stance. Like a knife slicing off the glitter on a performance or achievement. A title-slash.

A "you're *just* a runner" or "*just a father.*"

I didn't like it. But on some deeper level, I sort of understood it. Like "*just* finishing in the top ten at State."

I knew I wouldn't be satisfied with such a performance, given the goals, given the work. But still, there was some disconnect there.

I totally got the whole "be the best you that you can be" and all those lame inspirational quotes that sit in front of mountainous backdrops or the ocean with a curling wave. But when being the best you meant that it took you away from the people who love you (and you love), then what was the point of living that life?

That solo life?

Our achievements are to be shared. Otherwise, it's just you celebrating at Abo's Pizza. Alone. You can't high-five yourself without looking like an asshat.

I could finish in the top ten at State and not be satisfied, but I still had my friends and teammates and family. So while I would be pissed and likely drive up Boulder Canyon to Nederland on over to Estes to Lyons and back down to Boulder in a rage while listening to anything that fit my rhythm at the time, I still had people to share that emotion with.

I thought.

So why wasn't that enough for Dad?

Why wasn't he satisfied enough to be here with his wife and me? What was so bad about that?

I don't know where my mind went, but for a moment it was like the rankings didn't even matter, because Dad wouldn't even be around for the final product. I was studying for a test that would never come.

An anger boiled in my stomach, and I wanted to lash out at him while also soaking in every good moment we could have before he left again, for who knew how long. He could die over there from a heart attack and never return.

No.

I didn't want my last few days with him to be fueled by my frustrations. I knew that much. But at the same time I didn't know how to fully express what felt like a bomb stirring in my belly.

How could I fix this?

You can't.

Why not?

Because it's beyond you.

So what do I do?

Move along.

I reached NCAR and scanned the scene below, Boulder lit in a subtle orange glow. A gentle breeze danced with the trees, and I could feel the seasons changing beneath my feet.

Soon, everything would change. Again.

I stood in the dark along the trail so as not to be seen, so I could live in this moment fully. Without being perceived by anything or anyone. Just me. Here. Watching a million little lights twinkle beneath me. At night, it's always the holiday season.

The Boulder Bubble in all its glory.

That sweet mountain air filled my lungs, and I could smell autumn in Colorado. Like a candle filling the room. Crisp and full of transition.

From this distance the world was quiet, even though I knew life was bustling down on Pearl. But not here. With this gap of darkness between me and the world I could see more clearly. I could see every little speck, every little detail of what was, and what could be.

And I knew.

I'd have to go at this for myself. No one else but me. Because there was no purpose in chasing dreams for anyone else. That's a dog chasing its tail in circles.

I knew I couldn't change Dad's mind. Even my mom

couldn't. He was going to do whatever he wanted, however he wanted to do it.

And so should I.

In my way.

I'd rage on the course. Not for him, or anyone. Just me. I'd rage in my own way, at my own tempo.

Not because I had to or could. But because I wanted to.

The paintbrush was in my hand, and the 3.1 miles of dirt and grass would be my canvas. It didn't matter what the rankings said, or the fact that my father clearly didn't mind missing out on the biggest race of my life. Because rankings don't win races, and like all great achievements, I was doing this for me.

Two days later I watched my dad stand in the doorway waving with his big hairy hands while I headed off to school. I could've sworn his eyes were watering, but he rarely cried in front of me, and I was a solid fifty meters away on the sidewalk, so it was hard to tell. Maybe it was just the way the sun was hitting his eyes.

It was a moment that wasn't new.

I knew that when I got home that evening he wouldn't be there, and it'd be me and my mom, sort of.

She had a tendency to disappear when he wasn't around. So really this was them both leaving.

26

CLARITY

"What do you mean when you say 'it's quiet now'?" Lily was prying. Those deep brown eyes that made me feel warm and uncomfortable at the same time. That tiny wrinkle in her forehead. It was always hard to remain focused on her question. Maybe this is what Blake was talking about.

"It's. . . quiet. You know?" I spit out. Anything. Anything to keep this conversation going. We lingered in her driveway and I didn't want to go home yet. I looked back up that long cement slab toward the open garage and wished we were inside on that long couch in the downstairs TV room.

"Without your dad?"

"And my mom."

"What? Where did she go?"

Lily tilted her head a bit to the right, eyes beaming in curiosity. That classic Lily-look.

"I don't really know," I said. "I guess nowhere. She's still around, just not really present. You know?"

"You mean like she's distracted?" Lily said.

"Yeah. Something like that. Like, her mind is somewhere else. I'll go on rambling about this or that and look up and realize she's spacing out, lost in her thoughts or something. I think she's tired."

"Huh."

"And when I ask her if she heard me she closes her eyes and shakes her head with some half-ass apology then heads to her room really quick. I don't know."

It was strange explaining what life was like at home without anyone really there, but I hoped that maybe Lily would sort of get it, and then again, I was cautious with giving too much information. We were still a bit in that on-and-off thing, and I feared telling her too much would push her away.

What guy shares his heart fully without getting mocked at some point?

The last time I told a girl I was into her in a note she avoided me for weeks. She changed up her route to class entirely so she wouldn't have to walk by my locker, which is typically where I waited for her arrival. I'd pack my bag slowly, one book at a time, peeking over my shoulder, waiting for her to cruise around the corner with her blonde curls bouncing under that florescent high school light.

Months later her friend told me she thought there was something wrong with me. I'll never forget the look on her face—disgusted and full of pity. The way someone looks at dog shit on the sidewalk by their house.

"I'm a romantic!" I said in such a lame way before storming off. I went to the bathroom and hid in the stall for a few minutes fighting back tears.

What a loser.

Sometimes I wish I didn't have such a good memory, because remembering young Baxter is embarrassing.

Maybe there *was* something wrong with me.

"What does she do in her room?" Lily asked, eyes turning serious, a more curious brown but somehow still vibrant, like that slither of sapphire between the blues and purples of the evening sky.

"I don't know, but normally when she goes in there she doesn't come out. It's lights out for the night."

"So you guys don't eat dinner together like when your dad is around?"

For a moment it was like Lily was someone older than me, someone wiser, because I hadn't really considered what she was saying. She was clearly out-dueling me.

I searched for words in the air, an explanation for my lack of understanding or evading.

"I guess, I don't know. It's all just different. We just do our own things, I guess."

I really could play dumb and continue to pivot on this, because the truth was when my father was gone and it was just my mother and me we rarely spoke because we rarely saw each other.

"That's weird," she said.

"Yeah, it is, so maybe we should change the subject."

"Baxter, I'm trying to talk to you *about you.*"

"Okay, thanks. But I'm good."

Shut the door in three. . .two. . .one. . .

"I thought you wanted to talk *to me?*"

Now she was turning this thing around. Classic Lily style.

"I do."

"Are you sure? Because I could've sworn you were lingering in my driveway because you don't want to go home."

Okay. Now I was sure she could read straight through me. We always think we're more clever than we really are.

"Yeah," I said. "I just. . . I don't know. You're asking all this serious stuff, and—"

"You're the one who brought this up."

"Brought what up?"

"You said your house is quiet, or weird, all lonely like."

Busted.

"Okay. You're right."

"I don't want to hear I'm right. I just want to talk if you really want to talk. I want to *hear* you."

When did this girl become a woman?

"I get it—thank you." I put up the white flag, because the truth was I didn't want to go home. It was dark and cold and full of shadows.

My mother probably already locked in her bedroom after leaving a note on the stove on where to find leftovers.

But I couldn't tell Lily that.

27

WACKY DAY

IT WAS A TRADITION, EVEN IF JUST THREE YEARS OLD. When Coach came to Flatirons he brought a slew of odd quirks with him, like implementing "Wacky Day," which fell the week of Regionals, and required every member on the team to dress up in costume.

The first year we did this—my sophomore year—he failed to explain that whatever we showed up in for practice would be what we also ran in, so I donned a thick gorilla outfit of which the mask only had tiny holes for eyes and nostrils, and a tiny circular vent over the mouth. My sweat was trapped in this black carcass of plastic and dead hair while I trudged along the side of the road, holding on to a teammate's back because I could barely see out of the slits of eyes.

It was the longest, most grueling four miles ever.

Since then I had resorted to outfits that would be much easier to run in, like a girl's tennis uniform, Lily's, to be exact.

The short skirt wasn't too different from our Adidas

split shorts, though the sleeveless top was a little tight, but not tight enough to avoid being mocked by the football team when they grudgingly jogged by the track to the field.

"Look at that fag Baxter!" they woofed out, bellies spilling over their gray pants as if teenage obesity was the norm in Colorado.

Fortunately I wasn't too offended—I had long since gotten used to the fact that the physique of a male distance runner resembled that of most teenage girls, and for some reason simpler minds tended to associate male distance runners in short shorts—clearly for efficiency— to homosexuality.

The irony that most of those hood rats also indulged in donning tights and rolling around on a plastic mat together (wrestling) over the winter was never lost to me.

Their ignorance on the matter said more about them than me, so I often smiled and waved when they hurled their gibberish in my direction. Our disdain for each other was mutual, even if they couldn't comprehend it.

"All right, guys, gather around! Gather around!" Coach rallied the team, clipboard in hand. "You guys know the drill. You're voting for who you think has the best outfit, and no, you can't vote for yourself."

"That's okay, because we all know I'm gonna win over all you fools!" Tom laughed out, pointing his fingers like guns.

"Tom, in order to be in the running, you actually have to wear a costume. You're not even wearing a shirt," Coach shot back with a sly grin, knowing that with Tom there was always something. Like the time he lamely pole-danced at a green light until it turned red and he could cross the street. Or the time he chugged an entire bowl of hot salsa just to win a bet. Or the time he shaved his eyebrows to be more aerodynamic.

You get the idea.

"I don't have to wear anything," he said, pulling a wad of IcyHot out of his pocket. "Because I'm wearing this sh —stuff—on my nips! And my balls!"

He lathered his hands over his bare nipples and shoved them down into his pants, making a face of pleasure while the rest of us backed up in sheer disgust.

"No! No! No!" Coach scrambled to keep Tom from moving forward with his mischievous plan. "Tom! Tom! Stop! Stop that's not good!" He waved his hands but didn't get any closer to Tom than the rest of us.

"Too late, Coach, the deed is done!" he said, showing his bare hands devoid of any more IcyHot.

"You're crazy!" Blake said "Your balls are gonna be on fire any minute now!"

"Indeed they are. I can already feel the fire in my pants!" Tom screamed out, wafting the top out for air. "Ah sh—shoot—that's worse! That's worse!"

"Tom," Coach said, slowing his cadence down in a lower tone. "Tom, I need you to go to the bathroom right now, and wash everything you just touched."

"Why, Coach? This is my costume!" he pleaded. "I'm the IcyHot Man! So cool and so hot!"

"No, this is not a costume, and you could hurt yourself. I don't want your mother calling me again."

"Aw, come on, Coach! It's Wacky Day! And I'm just bein' wa-wa-wa-wacky!"

"Tom, seriously. Go to the bathroom right now, and wash all that off." Coach's tone went serious as he regrouped. "I can't have you doing anything that would hurt yourself, and like I just said, I don't want your mom calling me again every time you do this sort of stunt."

"Aw, Coach, you're no fun!" Tom said, waving him off as he trotted in short steps back to the locker room.

Coach turned back to the rest of us, who were holding in laughter, trying not to encourage Tom, but amused regardless.

"My balls are on FIRE!" Tom screamed over his shoulder, followed by a laugh.

"Okay, we're done with that. No more IcyHot for anyone." Coach shook his head while cracking a bemused smile. "Let's get back to business, we still have a run ahead of us, and everyone needs to vote. So, turn in your vote before you head out, and I'll get this tallied by the time everyone gets back."

The scent of IcyHot lingered in the air as we dropped our picks into Coach's navy blue Flatirons High hat.

Outside of Tom's theatrics, a freshman—Scotty—was a big-time favorite for the title. He must've been tipped off, because freshmen almost never came out of the gates swinging—they were usually thrown off by the whole ordeal. Usually Wacky Day was when they either decided to run cross country for the entirety of high school, or got so weirded out by our strange rituals they'd rather sit on the bench in clean white uniforms for junior varsity football games.

But Scotty clearly was one of us.

He wore a curly blonde wig, purple eye shadow, bright red lipstick, and what looked like his sister's prom dress from last year (his sister was hot, but well beyond any cross country runner's league.)

Running would his challenge, as the slit for the dress topped off around the knee, meaning he couldn't really lift his knees. The silver dress sparkled like tiny diamonds. He capped off the ensemble with white elbow-length gloves.

"If I had a hot sister who wore that sort of dress I could've pulled it off better," Todd said, clearly unsettled about being beaten out by a freshman.

"Only you would lament about not wearing a dress," Blake said, patting him hard on the back as we made our way out to the street.

And right there, their run was set.

Blake and Todd torched the first mile of our scheduled eight in just over six minutes. With Regionals just days away, I had every intention of reserving all of my competitive juices. It didn't matter what anyone was doing, or how fast they were running, I stuck to my own rhythm.

Besides, the tennis skirt was a little uncomfortable to run in, compared to half-slit running shorts.

28

SPAGHETTI DINNER

BASIL. BLACK PEPPER. BAY LEAVES. OREGANO. A little salt. Some sugar. And garlic. Mixed with tomato sauce and tomato paste. Add some water, filled just over the top of the ground beef, which was mashed to perfection before everything.

Mom's homemade spaghetti.

Those garlic and basil scents drifted through the house while the pot gently boiled. Mom had started making tonight's dinner a few hours ago.

"The longer it sits the better," she said while stirring, her green eyes scanning the contents of her creation.

I watched intently from the kitchen table.

I took notes with my eyes, jotting down every last detail.

Tonight was the final team spaghetti dinner, because within sixteen hours we'd all be going our separate ways, sort of. And, this being the last spaghetti dinner of the season, mom agreed to make her prized dish for the team.

The junior varsity ran in an unlimited race, so everyone not on varsity had their last shot for a PR, and the course was fast. For varsity, tomorrow morning would be judgment day of sorts.

We needed a top-two finish to guarantee our spot on the starting line of the State meet. A third or fourth place finish would send us to another week of racing at Sectionals, where we'd once again need a top-two finish, anything outside that and our squad would be done for the season.

For me, I wasn't exactly worried about making it to State—barring some insane disaster. A top-fifteen individual finish would get me to State, but that wasn't on my radar. I wanted a victory, which would add that coveted one point to the team score, which would only help our chances.

This time tomorrow we'd either be laughing over pizza and breadsticks at Abo's, or I'd be driving solo around town listening to Incubus with my windows down.

I'd either be going at this alone or with six teammates. It was a one-or-the-other sort of deal. Or that's how I looked at it, at least.

Mom's spaghetti boiled in tiny little bubbles while I eyed the pot, mouth watering, hungry now but waiting for a few dozen teammates to arrive. We also had breadsticks in the oven and parmesan cheese.

One by one the house began to fill. The doorbell rang every few minutes, or someone would just walk in, making themselves at home.

The arm of the couch became home to a variety of letter jackets and Adidas team jackets. Quickly, the house came to life, which was a big contrast to the past few weeks, which had been just me and mom.

Now, it was a living thing.

There was a mixture of moods, however.

In the dining room you could feel the tension of what was to come. Varsity guys wondering if tomorrow would be their last race. Todd worried that this would be it, being a senior and all. Blake not ready to end the season two weeks before the big show. The sentiment was even stronger for seniors on the JV squad, who knew this would be the epic finale of their high school career.

Like Ken.

Ken was perhaps one of the hardest workers on the team, but one of the least talented. Over the summer he showed up to every practice, and strained to run with the varsity guys. He never could hang, but watching him try really made me root for him. He had the right attitude, was willing to do everything to get better, but the magic just wasn't there.

I spent most of the season screaming at him in JV races, trying to urge him onto that next step where you release and find yourself on a new level, but no matter how hard he tried, he never did take that next step, and now he found himself outside the varsity, and a day away from toeing the line one final time.

My heart ached for him, but we both knew that he did everything he could, and this is where he was.

The best and worst part about running was that it never lied. You either did or didn't. It was a harsh truth, but at the very least, it was truth, which was much more than most of us get from the "real" world.

Ken sat solemn in the corner with his paper plate filled with spaghetti, and a breadstick on the side, eating quietly like he usually did.

I spied him from across the room and figured this would be my final chance for some encouraging words.

"You ready to go tomorrow, Ken?" I said.

He moved his spaghetti around the plate in anxiousness before taking a big gulp. Talking to Ken was always a bit of a struggle because he was never much of a conversationalist.

"Yeah, I guess so," he said, soft eyes looking up from his plate. He was a man going into battle, knowing he wasn't coming home.

"You've got this," I said, patting him on the shoulder. "All you have to do is what you've already done before. You know that."

"I know," he said, nodding along in his classic mellow way, eyes darting around the room, avoiding contact with anyone. "It's just. . ."

He paused in thought while I watched him search for his words in the darker corners of the room, perhaps beneath the table, on which sat all the food on display for the taking.

"It's just. . . I just wish I could go to State, at least once."

He let the word "once" fall low in tone, hopeless, like letting go of a dream he had long since chased, but had finally come to the realization that it was never going to happen. The harsh reality of running.

"I know, man," I said, shifting my energy to mirror his gloom. "I know."

"I'm content, I guess. I did everything I could. I believe that."

"I get it."

"It just wasn't in the cards, I guess."

We sat in silence for a moment, trying to navigate where to go next.

"If I can't go, you have to," he said, looking up. His words began to warm up, as his energy rose with the orange glow of the room. I could feel him shift in his seat. "I mean, you're going for both of us. I know you'll qualify, but if I can't go to Colorado Springs and race at Penrose, then you have to run for both of us."

I tried to decipher exactly what he was getting at, or what he meant.

"Okay, man." I nodded along, still slightly confused.

"I mean, my high school career ends tomorrow, and I wished it didn't, but it will. That's it. But yours won't. You have State. And so if I can't go, you have to, and you have to win, because you can."

And there it was.

"Sure, Ken," I said, mood shifting to something a little more serious. "I can—"

"No, Baxter, you will. You WILL," he said standing up from his chair, looking eye to eye with me now. "I did everything I could this season, and this is where it ends for me. But for you, you still have a little more in you. If I did everything I could, you have to as well. And I know you can win State. I know it. You have to know it too."

It was the most serious conversation I had ever had with Ken, but for once everything he said was starting to make sense. He was already a person of a few words, so when he spoke, it meant something. When Ken said something, you listened.

"I will," I said, locking eyes with him.

Tomorrow we go in to battle. And some of us aren't coming home.

For some of us, it ends. For others, it's another step toward a bigger goal.

PART III

29

REGIONALS

I STOOD ON THE STARTING LINE FACING WEST. SPIKES double-knotted, shaking my arms to loosen my shoulders, trying to bring myself to a yawn so I knew my lungs were all calm for the storm about to come.

I scanned the mountains that rolled and I thought about that conversation with Coach a few weeks back. Trees lined the various creeks along the course in various shades of yellows, oranges, and reds. The air was crisp in full autumn, or maybe that was the intensity of the day.

I hadn't raced since the dual meet, but my legs felt itchy to go. And I tried to remind myself that, rankings and previous results aside, I still had to qualify for State.

I stood in the middle of a field of nearly 100, feeling the tension linger in the air. Everything was on the line for *everyone*. Seasons would resume or die on this day. And while I was definitely eyeing a race beyond this one, I knew that with running, nobody gets a free pass.

The course at Stony Creek Golf Course was pancake

flat, or mostly flat when compared to the State course at Penrose.

This obviously changed the plan a bit. Given that there weren't any hills to really separate us, this would be all about a long, hard drive to the finish.

Coach and I had devised a plan that should secure a win, given no crazy curveballs.

Ryley Ohlson had been on a huge rise in recent weeks, per his usual curve, and while he wasn't inside the top ten state rankings, we knew better than to count him out. He was a kicker who reveled in championship-style races, which meant I'd have to rely on the one thing I had over him: strength.

So the plan was set.

Coast a mile with the pack—but keep the pace honest —then gradually push the pedal to the floor to string out the field, and with 800 to go, whether you have a shadow or not, it's lights out.

It's just another race, I was telling myself. You don't need a miracle. All you need to do is what you've already done: execute the plan.

When the gun shot out, everything felt like it was on cruise control. I didn't really have think, because my mind and body were already so in sync, I just had so be along for the ride, *a passenger.*

The pack took off hard, as usual, though I made sure to have some space and not fall—that would be perhaps the most possible of disasters.

We ran out, before looping back around to run through a tunnel of fans around the 1,000 meter marker. It was a sea of colors: reds, blues, purples. I couldn't hear a thing. Everyone on the sidelines knew what was at stake, and everyone on the sidelines was screaming bloody murder, because everyone on the sidelines knew just as much as everyone in the race, that every step would count for something.

I jumped to the front early to control the pace and the race. I was reluctant to let anyone change my plans, so I knew a nice honest pace from the get-go would discourage anyone else from going kamikaze.

After cruising through the wild tunnel we crossed a bridge and took a hard left to go out on the loneliest parts of the course—my favorite. I led a pack of a dozen through the opening mile as the clock ticked 5:07. . .5:08. . .5:09. . .

All right, time to shed some fat.

I gently pressed the pace to be somewhat noticeable, but nothing too crazy, no Tour de France-style attacks *yet*.

The pack thinned by halfway as we ran around a vast open field with fans screaming in the distance. The mountains loomed to the west, and I heard their call.

Come.

Ryley and Sean Roberson hovered over my shoulder, but I didn't mind. I wasn't thinking about them, I was thinking about each step, one by one, *forward*.

We looped around the open field and turned south around a tiny lake before a right turn led us down a long straightaway. I used every turn to drop a little surge, just a few steps to test the field, see where they were, see if they could respond, or if they were hanging on. We ran down the long straightaway before turning left to the only hill on the course, which led over a tiny creek.

I used the turn to glance over my shoulder and catch a

glimpse of the damage—it was just me, Ryley, and Sean with just over a mile to go.

Ryley and Sean seemed content in my shadow, as neither made any moves to attack. This meant one of two things: either they were sitting and waiting to attack, or they were holding on for dear life.

I leaned on the reality of the second.

After passing two miles we ran through another tunnel of fans before heading out for one final smaller loop. I really preferred the racing away from people, because it was when we were most alone, and we couldn't rely on anyone cheering to bring us up.

The strongest won in these times, because they didn't need anyone—they'd do it regardless.

Like Charlie Parker.

We cruised by the bridge—the next time we'd turn down it and straight for the finish—and away from all the noise and into the final mile. I surged hard now, as if revving up my engine before one final push—the final half mile.

I could sense the break behind me, as Sean began to lose a stride, then two, then three, and then it was down to two—me and Ryley.

We had raced four times this season, and this was the longest Ryley had been able to hang on, and despite this fact, I wasn't concerned.

I thought back to that dual meet. I thought back to the morning runs and half-mile repeats we had done right here on this very course, one I had come to know by the inches.

It didn't matter if he hovered in my shadow, because I still had something in my tank.

I tested him around each gentle bend in the course, and each time he responded, but the more I surged, the slower he responded.

We turned east for a few hundred meters before turning south and back on the larger loop, back toward the one gradual hill on the course, 800 meters to go.

Lights out.

Two weeks earlier I ran this final half mile in 2:18 at the end of six repeats with a two-minute rest. I was determined to touch that number even with two and a half miles in my legs already.

I tried to envision myself on a track and the bell ringing out for the final lap. This is where you get on your toes, where you put all of your cards on the table and set the house on fire.

I pumped hard, punching the air as if an invisible enemy was in front of me. The elastic band that kept us together began to stretch, and I could feel Ryley go from sitting to holding.

We took the final right turn of the course which led into the final 600 meters, a straight shot back to the finish line where the roar of the crowd awaited us.

I wished my father was in the crowd so I could hear the way he screamed "Baxter!" But I knew he wasn't here.

I listened to the fans on the sides of the course as they screamed for either me or Ryley, sensing how far back he was. Not much.

I couldn't feel him over my shoulder anymore, but I knew I wasn't alone on the trail. I knew he was tracking me, and would until we crossed the finish line.

I could see the bridge ahead, marking about 250 meters to the finish. I had run this final straightaway many times before, getting well acquainted with every last pebble. I knew that I could lose Ryley entirely at this turn if I surged through it, because there were two gentle turns in the final 250 meters, which would be enough for clear separation.

But I had to keep pressing.

For the first time all season I was in full flight and felt like there was still more in the tank. I had been kicking hard for nearly 600 meters now but felt like I had another 600, or 800, still in my legs.

I sprinted over the bridge and passed the horribly placed porta pottys. That scent of nervous shits in the air. Several hundred runners with spaghetti and breadsticks coming out the morning after.

I lifted onto my toes and felt my body move beyond my mind. A car without a driver—again, the passenger—everything moving without my force of will, as if it was all beyond me now.

I hit the final straightaway—that freshly cut grass (golf course grass is the best)—without a shadow. I had successfully run Ryley off my back and outside of my shadow. Now the Regional title would be mine.

I powered hard into the final meters, not trusting any lead, and across the line.

The bright red numerals ticked by 15:17.

Ticket to State: booked.

County: Check.

Region: Check.

Ryley finished six seconds later.

My hands fell upon the taped finish chute as I walked out the other end. My chest heaved up and down as I regained my composure. By the end of the chute I was breathing normally and turned back to see everyone else begin to file in.

We still had a team race on our hands.

Blake cracked the top seven—a good sign, but Todd and Chester were a half a minute back, not a good sign. I stood at the end of the chute, counting in my head before losing the tally.

And then the waiting came.

With Todd and Chester about a dozen or so places back from where Coach projected, anxiousness lingered in the air in such a contrast of emotions.

On one end I had just won my first Regional title, but on the other, there was the possibility that I might be headed to Colorado Springs without the guys I had spent much of the summer sweating out on the trails with, except Blake.

Blake shared the mixed bag of emotion. He qualified individually, but he, like me, was intent on *everyone* going.

He hovered by me, dipping between being ecstatic on qualifying—his first—and depressed that the team might not be joining us.

Meanwhile, Todd was lost in a gloom, staring at the finish line in a haze, worried that he might just have run his last race, while Chester was pacing and mumbling about next year.

It was inevitable that State favorite Niwot won the meet—they pumped five into the top fifteen. And then there was Fairview, who were a clear second, led by Ryley's runner-up finish. But third and fourth remained questionable.

Coach was busy tallying up on his notebook while we

mingled by our team tent, too nervous to even untie our spikes and go for a cool-down.

His nervous eyes went from left to right, up to down, and back to us while we all tried to decipher the look on his face.

"I'll be right back," he said, before jogging off toward the officials' table where every other coach was, trying to figure out whether to celebrate or conjure up some meaningful words to cap the season when delivering the bad news.

We watched in a trance from afar. Eyeing every last movement.

And then it came.

Coach turned from the table, clearly feeling our eyes on him. He looked up from his navy blue hat, and flashed a smile and a thumbs up.

But what place?

He jogged back over and let out a big exhale.

"Okay, guys," he started, still catching his breath. "So we're in."

We let out a few nervous cheers before he went on.

"So we're in—to Sectionals. *Barely*," he said. "We took the fourth spot, and eight points in front of Broomfield, so we live to run another day."

I let out a big exhale and high-fived the team. We knew we could get through Sectionals, and now I felt much better about going to State—the likelihood of having someone to share the experience with had taken a big shot of adrenaline.

With the news now concrete, the spikes came off, and Coach was back to the drawing board.

I switched out of my sweaty socks and laced up my

trainers as Coach came over, kneeling beside me as if to tell me a secret.

"You know what your last 800 was?" He asked.

"No—what?"

"2:15."

30

MOVEMENT

I STARED DOWN AT THE RED-AND-WHITE CHECKERED tablecloth and was nostalgic for a moment that hadn't yet passed.

That scent of pepper and pizza dough lingered in the air like a lit candle; it felt like home.

I could feel the pizza move down through my digestive system while my legs ached from the morning's pain session. Well worth it. And this was our prize. Two large pepperoni pizzas, breadsticks, and all-you-can-eat salads.

We had indulged in this ritual of post-meet pizza at Abo's for too many weeks to count, and it suddenly dawned on me that this would likely be the last time.

I sat back in the booth across from Lily and John, while we collectively marveled at Blake as he effortlessly and simultaneously entertained and amused us all.

"I totally got that Broomfield chick's number," he said, eyeing the cheese as it melted off his slice of pizza while shoving it in his mouth. "The hot one with the blue eyes."

"Which one?" John said, shooting a wide-eyed let's-mess-around-with-Blake look to me across the table. "I didn't see any hot girl with blue eyes."

John seemed intent on antagonizing Blake, but in a way much sweeter and less aggressive than Todd, who we collectively didn't invite to these post-race gatherings anymore. It always became a pissing contest between Blake and Todd.

"I told you," Blake said, taking a big gulp to clear his throat. "The Broomfield chick. The one with the blue eyes."

"You're gonna have to be more specific than that, Blake. There were a lot of girls with blue eyes from Broomfield. And are you sure she gave you the right amount of digits? Remember that one time."

"You always bring up that one time," Blame lamented.

"I have to," John said. "Someone has to *try* to keep you humble."

"Whatever. So do you know who I'm talking about or not?"

"I don't."

"The one with the ass," Blake responded with a big grin and a nod.

John shook his head in disapproval.

"So let me get this straight, you're asking me if I saw the girl from Broomfield with blue eyes and a nice butt?"

"I don't see where I lost you," Blake said, taking another slice off the pan.

"Blake, why do you always reduce girls to what they look like? Do you ever realize you sound like a dick?"

"Oh, come on!" Blake shot back, dropping the melted pizza onto his plate. "I was just describing her."

"Yeah, at least you started with her eyes *before* talking about her butt."

"One, it's ass, not butt. And B, how else are you attracted to a chick?"

"I don't know, Blake, maybe talking to her? Then you'll have more to go on than her *butt*."

"Okay, so before I get to talk to a chick, how do you know you'll like them? You—wait for it—have to be attracted to them first."

"He sort of has a point." Lily jumped in to break up the monotony of a two-person battle.

"See!" Blake said. "A girl's perspective! And she agrees with me!"

"Well, I said sort of." She rescinded her previous statement while sipping on her straw. Her brown eyes turned to amused, eyeing me from across the table.

I had no intention of breaking up their battle. I was stuck in the moment, soaking it all in, knowing that one day it'd all be gone.

"Okay, okay, but Lily *sort of* gets it," Blake said, getting the conversation back to a place where he could be right.

"Okay, Blake," John said, articulating his name. "So she gave you her number, she has blue eyes, and you like her butt. What else have you learned about little Miss Broomfield? Anything of substance? Or were the curves of her bottom all that you really cared for?"

"Okay, that was more than one question, so to answer them backwards, I *do* care for what she's got back there, and yes, I learned something of substance, that she's a long jumper who ran cross country to stay in shape for track—did you see her long tan legs? She could be a future engineer or a doctor for all I know. And then that's like the golden ticket right there. A hot chick who's smart. And, man, she's *in shape.*"

He nudged me with his elbow and laughed to himself while John shook his head, seeming ready to throw in the towel.

"You're crazy, man," I said.

"I know. And I know you guys enjoy it."

"Totally. I can live off your stories for another week."

Lily was checking her phone, keeping an eye out because her dad gave her a curfew since they were going to church in the morning. This meant no after-after-party for us, if there was an us. It was still such a weird thing, but I was forcing myself to just let whatever it was be and not define it. Every time I tried to define it she seemed to take a few steps back. Just let it flow.

Like running.

"You've got to go, don't you?" I said before she could even open her mouth with the bad news.

"Yeah, you know my dad—"

"Curfew!" Blake screamed. "Man that's gotta suck."

"Yeah, Blake, it does," she said, nodding with a sly smile before eyeing me. "Want to walk me out?"

"Aw, Baxter! Lily wants *you* to walk *her* out"! Blake was back to nudging my elbow, a little more aggressively this time.

"Shut up, man, and finish your damn pizza!"

We strolled into the night. The Flatirons were lit by the moon, and for a moment the stars spun around the earth a little slower. I could hear the transition of everything beneath my feet. Soon everything would be different, and we'd look back on this moment as just another memory, another piece in the puzzle of a picture we could not yet see.

When we got to her car she jingled her keys to find the right one, a nervous tick.

"So," I started, curious if we'd be capping this night with a kiss, a hug, or a see-ya-later. "Thanks—uh—for coming."

"Yeah, thanks for inviting me."

"Well, extra thanks because I know you don't really like those guys."

"I don't mind them. Blake is a little much sometimes."

"Yeah, he's always much," I tried to joke, but was sure she could see right through my nervous tick.

We stood in that awkward silence, unsure of what to do. Who takes the lead here? Do I lean in for a kiss? Or just say "Bye, girl" and walk off?"

"Well, this is awkward. . ." she broke the silence.

"Uh. . . yeah. . . sorry."

"Don't be sorry, Baxter," she said looking up at me, big brown eyes evening the shadows of the night. "So, are you going to kiss me or what?"

"Do you *want* me to kiss you?"

"Baxter, you're such a dork sometimes."

Half an hour later I zoomed back and forth on the winding road up Flagstaff Mountain. After the morning's race, the fun at Abo's, and some lip-to-lip action with Lily, I didn't want to go home where everything felt stagnant. I needed to *move*.

I drove with the windows down, letting in that crisp mountain air that was cooling by the night. My fingers dangled as the wind sliced between them. I inhaled layers of pine while climbing up into the mountains, back and forth, back and forth, back and forth up that winding road in the dark, listening to Dave Grohl and that speeding tickle of the high hat blare out of my speakers.

"Breathe out, so I can breathe you in."

My mind raced.

The day had felt like two or three with everything that had happened. And I wasn't ready shut my eyes on it just yet. I needed to process everything, refile, and reassess where to go with everything.

What was next?

The headlights from my car sent out a long wave of light into the road in front of me, barely enough to light up the way, but I had done this drive many times before —I had run up this road. I was familiar with the turns.

The night was dark, but I paid no attention. My mind was in front of me, like earlier when I raged across the course as a passenger. And now even off the course I felt like a passenger while driving my own car, a passenger in life. Like the ball was already rolling down the hill in one direction and I had no power to stop it. Somewhere long ago I had started this movement in whatever direction this was, and now the ball was rolling faster and faster, and I could nearly see a destination, or a checkpoint. It was all leading somewhere, but I didn't exactly know where. Everything was happening so fast, or so it felt, even in this moment where nothing had really changed at all. Not yet.

Everything was in flux, even if it didn't look like it. I could feel it like the wind you can't see.

I sensed a wave, or perhaps a tsunami coming, but I couldn't yet figure out whether that was a good thing or a bad thing. It was a sense of change, like the seasons.

There's always that gentle wind that comes first at the change of summer to fall or winter to spring, where it feels a bit different, warmer or colder than everything else.

I drove on into the night, unsure of when or where I'd turn around. I intended to drive until whatever this urge was taking me this way prompted me to turn and go home. But it felt like for the first time in my life, I was in sync with everything, doing what I was supposed to do, at this exact time.

31

SHARPENING THE MIND WITH A KNIFE

A GOLDEN GLOW HOVERED OVER THE BEIGE PAGES. IT lessened the strain on my eyes a bit, and it added a bit of drama to the whole ordeal of reading at night.

I sat propped up on my bed while the rest of my room lay hidden in the shadows. Not visible was the row of muddy running shoes by the door. The heap of running shorts and shirts in the corner, all clean, and all in their rightful place, in a mountainous bundle on the floor. The clean white sheet with **"WIN STATE"** written in bold lettering that sat just above the light switch so I'd have to see it every morning and every night.

But for this one moment, nothing out there mattered, because what was right in front of me was one of the most important building blocks for everything out there.

I was reading Parker Christie's *Edge Runner* for the sixth time in the last two and a half years. The pages were riddled with various earmarks from the many reads, the occasional underlined passage or phrase that prompted philosophical thought on the matter, and the cover, that original maroonish watercolor with a shirtless runner with shaggy hair looking down was beginning to crack. The runner almost looking blurred and ominous, like it could be anyone since the details were lost in the soft curves.

Reading it the final weeks of the season had become a ritual of sorts. It had become as important as eating spaghetti the night before a race, or double-knotting your spikes, or hanging up your singlet with the race number already pinned.

I read *Edge Runner* a week and half before whatever race I was peaking for and once over winter break. It stood in same important cycle as winter or spring or summer break.

I had timed it to sync with finishing it the Thursday before a Saturday race, which left Friday to think about Saturday. It was the perfect pick-me-up, surpassing even Survivor's "Eye of the Tiger," the Foo Fighters' "My Hero," or even Cake's "The Distance." And the list goes on. There was no song that conjured more motivation than "Edge Runner."

As great as those songs all were, or are, they only added a momentary race of blood pumping through my body.

Edge Runner did that and more—it reset my mind, reminded me what I was doing all of this for, almost like scanning the pages of my training journal, but adding a witty narrative and plot to it to make it all feel more real.

Coach had suggested the title over winter break my sophomore year as something to get me through the colder, lonelier weeks of training. I hadn't ever read any running-related fiction or non-fiction before, and paled at reading in general, but after the opening chapter I was hooked.

I read the book cover to cover in three days, and when I put it down, I picked it right back up to read it all over again.

It was that good.

When I came out the other end, I was a different runner. Call it what you will, but the best description is *enlightened.*

It made me feel like I like I wasn't alone out there, or anywhere. There was a club or a squad or a group, and even though I was pursuing something as individual as distance running, I was a part of it. At the time, this was new territory. Like owning a Members Only jacket in the eighties and seeing someone else with the jacket on the street, you're both part of this quasi-cool club, or so you think, even though you bought your jacket separately. Like a badge of honor that very few knew or understood, a secret community of skinny oddball personalities spanning not just the country or the world, but time and space. The strange personalities in the book resembled some of the strange personalities I knew and occasionally shared sweat with on the trails. It was a mirror into my own life, but with the names and dates and courses or tracks changed.

Racing the morning run was generally held with disdain, like showboating your talents when the pack knew who the alpha was on the course.

And all this time I thought I was alone.

Good books, like good songs, make you feel like you're not alone in your thoughts and pursuits, and *Edge Runner* did that for me.

It was like reading about a fictional dream of mine. We were all Ryan, or Mike, in some form or another. And I definitely knew a Gordo or two.

It put me in the right frame of mind to do what I had set about doing months earlier on the trails when I daydreamed about such lofty goals or ambitions.

Reading *Edge Runner* within ten days of the big race was like peaking.

It was peaking.

I sifted through the pages, left to right, memorizing where I saw a word or a phrase along the way. I could recite it without reading a word, going chapter to chapter. Like the course at Penrose, I knew all the curves and hills along the way.

Call it an obsession, call it what you will, it almost always worked.

The previous spring I had finished third in the 3200 at Regionals, missing a State qualifier by two seconds, and one place. Last fall I finished fourth at State, despite not being ranked in the top ten heading to Colorado Springs. The spring before that I took on the region in in the 3200 as a sophomore, leading five laps of eight before dying a thousand horrible deaths and crawling home to finish sixth.

Almost.

What *Edge Runner* did to my mind was set it in a place to attempt big things. It was like a shot of adrenaline in the tiny arm of a distance runner where it's close enough to hit bone, or if you could chug down confidence or courage from a water bottle. It was a performance-enhancing vitamin, but in the form of words and story.

All I had to do was train my body to respond to this boost—and the past month had proven my body was ready to roll, now more than ever.

And now with Sectionals this week and State the next, it was time to sharpen my mind with a knife.

Slice into a dagger that could take down anything or anyone, even a damn vampire.

It was time.

32

WHO'S MORE NERVOUS?

"How are you feeling?" Coach said between breaths.

Since Regionals was behind us, that left just the Varsity, which meant he could run with us rather than hang back with a clipboard and make sure the JV guys weren't getting into any trouble.

"I'm feeling good," I said.

"Just good?" He prodded like a scientist.

"Better than good, almost great, but not great, but better than good," I said in one long exhale as we strode along the single-track trail on a portion Blake had called "Baxter's World," since it was my favorite two-mile stretch of trail in the area. This was typically where I'd throw down the hammer, using the single-track trail the way mountain bikers do, running the turns, leaning into gravity to let it take me off and away. And I always got carried away here.

But not when I ran with Coach. When I ran with Coach, I ran *with* Coach. There was never a need to surge away from him, he ran with you to get a better feeling of how the training was affecting us. In-season, there was always a scientific purpose if he ran with you. Out of season, well, we'd talk more about The Smashing Pumpkins or Weezer than running.

"Okay, so good," he said, hopping over a fallen log I had hurdled like a steeple in an overly dramatic style as if it were higher. I had more pep in my stride than usual, the effects of peaking right in time, and I had to do something with this energy or explode.

"Careful, Baxter," he said, shaking his head. His long mechanical arms swung back and forth, driving him forward.

"What?" I continued to stride down the trail like a mountain biker, rolling up and down and popping off slight corners where the trail cut from a few tree roots.

"You know what."

"What?"

"Baxter, just don't hurt yourself."

"Coach, that log was like two feet off the ground."

"I know, but you didn't know what was on the other side."

"Yeah, I did. I've run here hundreds of times."

"Okay, I'm not going to argue that, just please, please be careful. We're too close."

"Okay, I get it, I get it." His case was valid. When he said the words "We're too close" the frame of the conversation shifted from "don't play around" to "don't play around and get injured because State is next week." Okay. I get it.

"We've just got to keep you healthy for another eight days."

"Just eight?"

"You know what I mean."

Coach cared for his athletes like a father his children or a scientist his experiment. He wanted to control all the variables, not so much for the sense of control, but because he cared deeply for what he did, and for us. In some sense, we were his kids. And me? I was his oldest. Pet Project Number One ever since that run over two years ago where he asked about my goals for the future. And now suddenly we were just days away from the culmination of it all.

In that sense, yeah, I understood why he was nervous.

It wasn't just me on the starting line, it was us. He had shared much of the brunt of the work with me, even if not on the track. It was his fevered mind coming up with the workouts, tinkering here and there every time something didn't add up correctly. And in the off-season, we shared miles and conversations.

It wasn't just *my* goal to win State, it was *ours*. Because he had invested in this task just as much as me.

We ran on in silence for a bit, hidden beneath the trees that stretched upwards toward the sky. Tiny little pines that lined the trails made a softer surface. We danced over tiny roots that stuck out, making it a little more challenging to run fast.

"This is why I preferred a road-route, even the dirt road," Coach said, clearly nervous. He slowed the pace and kept his eyes down at the terrain while I hopped from one side of the trail to the next. I had run this trail so much I could do it eyes closed, and even teased Coach with the idea, but he wasn't up for games, and he had a good point.

. . .

"Aw, come on, we've done too many workouts on the dirt road," I said. "And the roads are scary too—drivers come real close to side-swiping, sometimes they even spit."

We continued our descent downwards along the winding trail, back to school from the Flatirons that we left behind us now.

"They spit?"

"Totally."

"You never told me this."

"I know. It was just some kids."

Light blue truck. Key scratch down the side. Five kids. Fleshy pale kid in the passenger seat in the back. Bleach-blond hair. Freckles. Maybe a junior. Probably sophomore since he's in the back—can't drive. White t-shirt. Country music blaring. Pure white-trash look about him. Leaned out the window. Puckered up. Hurled a wad a spit as we crossed paths down Table Mesa Drive. Perfect aim. A few honks and laughter while I turned to give them the finger. Totally thought about chasing them to the red light to give them a scare. Then realized they'd likely kick my ass —butt. I *am* a distance runner.

"Some kids spit at you?"

"Bullseye on the chest."

"You're *not* serious."

"Totally am. It was actually quite impressive."

"You're *not* serious."

"No—I am."

"Baxter, you should have told me sooner."

"Why?"

"Why?" He chuckled. "Because this is the kind of

thing to bring to the Athletic Director to make sure you guys are protected."

"Protected? Like we get some bodyguards or bouncers?"

"No. Just so they can send out a PSA."

"So I should've told you about the beer bottle?"

33

SECTIONALS

It was strange to toe the line at Sectionals, already thinking about State. As if this was some formality in the way of something bigger (it was), but in waiting for the starter to get this shindig going, I realized the butterflies that typically swarm in a rage in this moment weren't fluttering at all. They were dormant, sleeping as if this was no big deal at all. Barely a workout. *This?* This was a shakeout.

And then another realization came to me: my lack of enthusiasm for this race had everything to do with how far I'd come from getting torched in the final 200 meters by Vince Charles at the Stampede—because he was on the line just a few steps away, doing the same thing I was doing. Trying to help get his squad to State.

Though we entered this day and the coming week from two entirely different paths.

On one hand, he had taken a nosedive since winning the Stampede, which wasn't too much of a shocker. Vince always ran summer track, late into August, so when the cross country season arrived he was always on the tip of peak shape. Then as the season progressed he'd gradually take a few steps backwards as the sharpness from turning left softened.

Meanwhile I was taking leaps forward.

And while it did linger in my mind a bit that he had lit my ass on fire at the Stampede, something inside me told me that we weren't in the same league anymore.

And so the butterflies remained snoozing well after the gun went off.

By the mile marker I had shed every shadow, even Vince. He didn't really seem concerned with the giving chase. He seemed content with taking two points in the same way I was content with taking one.

I cruised over the course—the same one from Regionals—like it was a post-race victory lap. There was a sense of déjà vu but lacking any of the emotion from the previous week. There was no Ryley hovering around, trying to play the spoiler.

I ran well within myself, saving up my last penny for next week. Today was all about getting that one point so I could stand next to my six teammates at Penrose next week. One point. That was all that mattered.

So I tempoed.

After cruising through the opening mile in 5:09 with Vince a few strides back, I pushed the pedal a bit because I felt like I wasn't even breathing. And because I didn't really feel like running with anyone.

I loved racing when in peak form, because everything felt easy unless you were truly racing to your abilities. You could shift gears with efficient precision. Like everything was lubed and smooth, like a bike with many gears and unlimited quad strength to manage it all.

Mile two came and went with a 4:57 clocking, and still I felt like I had plenty of gears in my legs. Somewhere behind me Vince was struggling, and in his struggle Blake was eating up the precious space between them with each giant stride he took. If he didn't run out of real estate, claiming Vince's skull would be a huge run for Blake.

I soloed into the final mile, focusing on a nice, even-keeled stride, something bordering on effort, but well under control. I listened for anything behind me, but all I could hear were the quick footsteps of my spikes over the freshly cut grass and my steady breathing. For a moment, I reminisced back into the summer months when I'd tear around the trails, and the only sound was my breathing and the crunch of dirt beneath my clunky trainers.

Back in this moment, I kept the red-line in front of me. I kept each stride well under control.

No need to spend all my money at a second-hand thrift store.

I cruised over the gradual hill, the same one I had used to separate myself from Ryley a week earlier, and back toward the finish, where the mountains sat as a perfect backdrop to this glorified tempo run.

I took giant strides over the bridge so as to not waste any spike time on the wood, and passed the badly placed porta pottys to the left, this time not smelling nearly as vomit-inducing since there weren't as many teams, so less shit to stink up the makeshift plastic bathroom with.

I eyed the clock but didn't kick in as I entered the final straightaway. I maintained as if this was sending a message of its own. Today the message wasn't the time nor the place but the effort.

And the effort took me across the line in 15:29.

And it felt *easy*.

I had sets of mile repeats and tempo runs that felt harder than that. What was that saying? *A walk in the park?*

Yeah. It was something like that. The ease with which the time came was encouraging, given that it wasn't much slower than last week, and that I spent nearly every step of those 3.1 miles with the weight of next week drifting around in my mind. Yeah. I'd take it as a *good* sign.

But now all my attention turned behind me as I walked through the finishers chute, breathing already back to normal.

When I turned I could hear a race real going on, so I rushed out of the chute and around to the side where I could cheer.

Vince was holding off a late-charging Blake, who was red-lining hard for this scalp. It was the kicker versus the upstart, and when they neared the line it was clear that Blake would run out of precious real estate, but damn he had a *great* run—Vince, while not the Vince from August or September, was still a top-ten kind of guy at State. He was ranked seventh as of this morning, not that I checked. But I did.

If Vince was a top ten kind of guy, then so was Blake based on this performance.

Vince tore into the chute with Blake just a stride back. Vince looked gassed, while Blake's fatigue quickly shifted to elation when he realized he'd finished third—and just a stride behind Vince.

Blake held onto the strings that lined the finishers' chute and made it out, taking heavy breaths. I ran over to congratulate him but he beat me to the first line.

"Did. You. Just. See that?" he asked between breaths.

"Yeah, dude! You almost had Vince Charles!" I said, hands on his shoulders shaking him.

"Okay, don't. Do. That," he said "I think. I'm gonna. Puke."

He stumbled over to the black trashcan and proceeded to empty out the contents of his stomach, likely that jalapeño burrito I couldn't believe he ate for breakfast and last night's spaghetti.

Who eats a jalapeño burrito for breakfast?

And Blake wasn't the only one to have a great run.

Todd and Chester came in as a pair in sixth and seventh, giving us four in the top seven, and John capped out our scoring with a fifteenth-place finish.

We didn't need to add anything up to know we clearly had a State-qualifying run. We won that race outright.

There was no gloomy wait-and-see this week. This week we paced quickly over to the team tent sharing battle stories from the race just minutes old, knowing that we'd all be headed to Penrose for the Big Dance.

Sure, it took Sectionals to get us there, but it didn't matter how we got there. We got in. And now everything. All aspects of life. Everything. Everything shifted to State. There were no more big races in between now and then. No more death-defying workouts to make gains with. There were no more questions.

Well, maybe one.

And that was how to manage my nerves over the next six days.

34

MONDAY

I couldn't keep still.

My legs were anxious, shaking, bolting with energy constantly. Peaking was a whole other challenge. It was all about controlling all this excess energy.

The past two Sundays were devoid of the typical twelve to thirteen-mile long run and replaced with six miles.

Six miles?!

Cutting my Sundays in half left a reserve of energy, and I was feeling it now sitting in Mrs. Blake's class.

The noise outside my head was one giant roar of white noise with no distinct voices. I was lost somewhere in the jittery sensations of peaking when everything went silent.

I looked around, confused, and saw Mrs. Blake—and the entire class—looking at me.

"What?" I said, scared for a moment that I'd shit myself or was talking to myself without even noticing.

"I said, are you with us, Mr. Reeves?" Mrs. Blake said with a slightly annoyed tone.

She said my name.

"Uh, yeah—yes—I'm here."

"Okay, good, because I'd like for you to read your last paper to the class," she said, with a wink. This was part of the extra-credit she was *allowing* me to do to get a better grade. *Dammit.*

I'd have to earn it.

"Uh, you want me to read out loud?" I started shuffling through my notebook for the paper I had written Sunday night while watching *Ridiculousness* in the background.

"Yes, Mr. Reeves."

I fumbled around for what felt like an eternity, trying to find the earmarked paper. I couldn't control my hands or my feet. Soon I had something in my hands, and my feet were a few steps ahead of my mind, already standing up and moving toward the front of the class.

"You don't have to stand to read," Mrs. Blake said. "You can stay seated if you prefer. It's up to you."

I quickly took a 180 and plopped nervously back in my seat, clenching my paper, causing wrinkles in the process.

"Uh, okay, Mrs. Blake."

I was an entirely different person in the class compared to the course, and now Mrs. Blake was putting a big spotlight on that glaring fact, because I'd read out my recap of the race. The one where I torched the field, didn't care, and coasted to victory like a badass.

But I didn't feel like that here in her class. I felt like a fly on the wall that anyone could squash if they gave a look.

"Okay—I—ugh—I—ugh. 'I knew the race was over as soon as the gun went off.'"

That white noise rang in my ears. I couldn't even hear my own voice. I just read off the lines one by one in a trance, reliving the race for a moment. I couldn't feel anyone's eyes on me now, because I wasn't here. I was on the course, dropping Vince with ease, and then back around the lake. *Cruisin'.*

When I looked up everyone sat wide-eyed, and I had a quick flashback to just moments earlier when I was lost somewhere in my own thoughts when Mrs. Blake turned the light onto me.

Did she even ask me to read? Was I really here?

For a moment I panicked. I tried to replay the last few minutes in my head to clarify if Mrs. Blake did ask me to read, or if I just in some manic moment saw something in my mind that didn't actually happen.

Add the bolts of lightning trickling through my veins. This must be what it feels like to truly be crazy.

"That was *great*, Mr. Reeves," Mrs. Blake said, letting the word "great" linger, while flashing that white-toothed smile that every guy in class swooned over. Her right eyebrow rose in amusement while she stood, arms behind her back, eyeing me intently.

Yes, Mrs. Blake.

"You can leave that on my desk," she said, turning and making her way back to the corner of the class. "And good luck this weekend."

I could feel a giant exhale leave my body involuntarily. I had survived, whatever that was. I hadn't been here, or even thinking about being here, so everything in the world felt like a curveball.

My mind revolved around the day's workout, not anything else.

The rest of the day went this way. Me, jittering in my seat, legs constantly shaking, bouncing nervously under the desk. Me, hoping that no one noticed. Me, eating a salad for lunch because it felt like all my stomach could keep down.

I'd been on the starting line plenty of the times this season and didn't feel this nervous. But now, with no long runs in my legs and the biggest race of my life just days away, everything felt like I was just waiting for the starter to shoot the gun and send us out of our misery.

I hadn't fully noticed how much of a mute button my long runs had been until now. They'd level me off Sundays, putting some lead in my legs. By Tuesdays I'd feel a little better, but then we'd have our workout, putting lead back in the legs. Thursday we'd do this all over again, and by Saturday we were typically racing.

Now there was no mute button to set the tone for the week.

I couldn't get tired—nothing took the edge off. It was *all* edge now.

The afternoon set of 6x400 repeats came and went without a hitch. It all felt like a formality at this point.

"We're just sharpening up," Coach said after giving out final instructions.

He put a cap on speed until the final one to make sure no one could get injured. This meant a very controlled 66-second quarter with a minute rest that I ran like clockwork. I didn't need a watch. I would count out my strides and run any pace between 64 and 70 seconds down to the hundredth of a second. I could feel the difference between a 69 second quarter, and a 68, or a 70, or a 66, or a 64. I once even bet Coach that I could do this without a watch—and won.

Sixty-six second quarters on tap with a minute recovery. Yeah—*I mean yes.*

I did my ritual of a figure eight worth of a walk in that minute around the starting line before lining up again, left foot on the line, eyes down, focused, ready to get back to business. By the time Coach would click the watch to start the next interval, I was able to yawn.

After five 400s anywhere between 66.1 and 66.6 I felt as fresh as I did at the start of the workout.

Nothing could make me tired.

"Last one. Keep it controlled," Coach said in a stern voice, still managing his horses, his dark eyes hiding beneath the long brim of his hat. He was just as nervous this week as we were but couldn't release that energy out on the track like us. That must've been brutal. "But let's see what you've got in your legs."

That was a green light.

When he clicked the watch I tore off around the top of the track, leaving everything behind. Down the back straightaway I pumped hard, feeling the intensity of the workout for the first time of the day. It felt *good* to stride out and let loose. A mustang reaching vast fields without a tree or fence in sight.

At the 200 mark I leaned into my stride as if starting a new interval. Around the final curve and into the straightaway I maintained my cadence, careful not to teeter over the edge, but keeping everything rolling. I had been numb to every effort for over a week now, and I yearned to feel *something*. Something that tasted like blood in the mouth.

58. . .59. . .60. . .

I had never broken 60 for a 400 before.

Not until the sixth and final quarter of the day when I cruised by in 59.7.

Four days to go.

35

TUESDAY

"Don't use it all, man," Blake said with his head over the sink. "If you use it all your hair will be *bleached*."

He rubbed the blue coloring deep into his scalp while I did the same with blonde hair dye from the bathtub. Blue streaks ran down his arms and onto the sides of the sink, far from their intended final destination.

I could still hear my father's judgmental tone—"Baxter, clean up this mess"— echoing inside my mind. That constant nag. A voice that always made you look in the mirror. So overly conscious that it put a roadblock to any sort of free-flowing thought or action.

It was always easier to be a bit more rebellious when he wasn't around. The cuffs were off.

The positive side of my father being halfway across the world was that he wouldn't be around to berate us about the mess we were making.

It'd be long wiped down and cleaned up before he got back.

It had become a tradition of sorts, like spaghetti dinners, to dye our hair blue for State. But with my dark brown locks, I figured the blue wouldn't show unless I dyed it blonde first, then blue. Last year the blue came out dark and was only visible when the sun scorched the tips of it. It had this metallic-blue hue to it.

Senior year. I was determined to have the same shade of blue as everyone else on the team with lighter hair.

#TeamPride

And so here I was, leaning over the tub to keep the mess contained to something that would be easier to clean afterwards. Step one of the process was the blonde dye, which I'd have to leave in for a day, then go blue. So I rubbed excessively at my scalp and down the curly locks to ensure that every last strand was getting the goods. I could feel every last inch of my head turn to fire as the toxins soaked in, bleaching my hair and my brain.

And then, I waited, my head wrapped in a ball of heat. Blake and I sat on the couch, aimlessly flipping through channels while we waited for the proper amount of time to pass before unleashing our creations. Dried rivers of blue streaked down the sides of his face.

A for effort.

"I'm so pumped for Saturday," Blake said, eyeing the TV while I flipped through the channels, one to the next.

"You should be," I said. "You had a *big run* at Sectionals. You *can* get Vince at State."

"Well, that's the goal," he said, shifting his tone to an analytical one. Coach really had created a team of students of the sport. "If I can just keep him in distance, I might be able to kick him down this time."

"Totally."

"I just have to not let him get too far ahead, like Sectionals. He had nine seconds on me heading into the last mile, and six of those in the second mile."

"It's the second mile that'll make the difference," I agreed. "If you keep him around through the middle mile, you'll find something the last mile. Everybody does."

We sat in silence while both of us daydreamed away from the couch and onto Penrose, some 100 miles south of where we were sitting at in this very moment. It was hard to stay still in the same spot that week—mentally, that is. You could be sitting on a couch or at a desk or in your bed, but your mind was off somewhere in the clouds, somewhere in a different space and time. Living another moment well before it happened.

I had done this for years. I'd run a race in my head a thousand times before ever stepping foot on the course or the track. I had done this for State too many times to count, playing out every last scenario, every possibility, and what I would do.

What if Grant Hemingway went out hard from the start? Hang on and let him die out himself, then counter. What if Grant Hemingway hammered after a mile? Tuck in and wait for the last mile to counter. What if Grant Hemingway sat and waited to kick? Torch his ass over the last mile. What if Grant Hemingway was still around for the final kick? You'll find something, you always do when it matters the most.

I had won this race so many times in my head already. It was almost like a memory now.

A mile's worth of time later Blake sat up and touched the towel that wrapped over his head, making sure everything was still in place.

"What about you?" he said, looking over at me as if goading me into the conversation.

"What about me?"

"Come on, Baxter, don't divert," he said. "How are you feeling about *everything*?"

"Everything?" I tried to pivot away from the topic. Because the reality was my stomach had been twisted all week. Talking about it only made it worse. It was painful. I was already thinking about it more than enough, and talking about it just felt like daggers in my stomach, and the butterflies had to swarm around to evade.

Blake gave me an eat-shit look that I couldn't escape.

"If I'm excited, I know you are, and I'm nervous, and I know you've got to be too."

"I feel *good*," I said. "Great, actually."

"Good, man, that's real good." He nodded. I could feel his excitement, and it was already too much in addition to mine.

"I'm just nervous man, I just—talking about it makes me really nervous."

"I get it," he said, taking a pause. "But sometimes talking about it can help you get it out, you know?"

"Not really. Do you know my family?"

We laughed for a moment before he continued.

"No, really, you've got to get some of that anxious stuff out, otherwise it'll eat at you," he said. "And you need to save all the good stuff for the course, for Saturday."

He had a point.

"When did you get so wise?" I teased. It was hard to take him seriously while he had dried blue dye twisting down the sides of his face.

"I don't know. People underestimate me."

"I can't imagine why."

"Whatever, Baxter! I'm being serious."

"Oh, I can tell."

"No, I mean I'm being serious that you've got to calm your mind. You've got this. You're going to win State. I believe it, really."

"You really think that?"

"Totally. You're the craziest guy I know—and I mean that in a good way, like you're so damn competitive. You figure out how to win races because you get into everyone's head. You understand the guys that don't understand themselves, and then you go to work on them. It's time to get your crouton man…"

Somewhere over the many miles on the trails or playing Xbox at Blake's house, I had found someone who knew me.

Or maybe it was the toxins leaking into our heads.

36

WEDNESDAY

"Just one more." Coach said, writing times from the third 200 on his clipboard.

"Wait, one more?"

"That's what I said, one more."

"So just four 200s?" I pried. This couldn't be true. Only four?

"It's good to see you can count," he joked, nodding and herding us back to the starting line. "I want to keep you guys fresh and ready for Saturday, so just four today, okay?"

Four 200s felt like a 100-meter warm up, not enough to really get loose. The warmup was longer than the workout. But Coach knew what he was doing.

We nodded in unison and lined up three wide.

"And nothing crazy, I don't want anyone running faster than 28 seconds, Baxter."

"Oh, come on."

"Nope. I want this under control, no crazy stuff. This is just to make sure you guys are nice and loose. Ready?"

Coach stood inside the track with his hand in the air, holding the stopwatch high the way a starter raises his gun.

The seven of us gently leaned forward, waiting for Coach to send us off into our fourth and final 200. For a second I could feel the intensity in the air like just before a race launches off the starting line, where time feels eternal, where everything stops, just for that one moment. We hung there in this moment, waiting, waiting, waiting, and then he sent us off.

I coasted across the white line of lane one 28.01 seconds later. Coach continued to read off as the time clicked on, 29. . . 30. . . 31. . . then scribbled quickly on his clipboard.

We slowed to a trot then a walk, feeling like not much had just transpired. Just another day's work.

"All right, spikes off, get your trainers on and just one for everyone," Coach said, placing the clipboard beside his navy blue jacket. "And I'll join you."

We jogged down toward the lake for the one-mile loop where we had endured plenty of repeats and tempo runs. The Flatirons loomed tall in the distance, the Boulder running gods watching over us. We had paid our respects on the track, so we could proceed. Pockets of yellows and oranges were scattered over the hills and mountains above us. Soon they'd all be colorless twigs. Skeletons of their former selves.

I hung near the back of the pack, soaking up every opportunity to be lazy. Soon I wouldn't have this option, but in the final days, everything felt easy, and everything *was* easy. Somewhere up ahead Blake and Todd were in their usual bickering about girls or nonsense, John teased and laughed and poked at them both, while Chester ran on in his own mind, counting the minutes when he'd be back underneath his girlfriend.

Coach ran in stride with me, launching into his general probing of our progress.

"Everything feeling good?" he asked as if he didn't know the answer, those questioning eyes hiding underneath the brim of his hat.

"I think that 28.01 sort of answers that question, right?" I said with a laugh.

"I just want to make sure it *felt* easy," he said, emphasizing his point.

"It felt like a 34," I joked.

"Good," he said, letting the moment simmer for a bit. "I had to make sure those toxins hadn't bled into your brain and fried everything we've been working on."

He nudged me with his bony elbow and laughed.

"Is it that bad?" I asked, touching the dried blonde locks of my hair.

"Let's just say it'll be better when you dye it anything other than blonde."

"So it's that bad."

"Mrs. Blake even mentioned how it wasn't a good look."

"No."

"Yes."

"Maybe the blue will look better when I dye it tonight."

"Probably not, but it doesn't matter what color your hair is Saturday, because we've got a race to run."

"I'm feeling *good*."

"Like good, or really good?" he prodded, back into scientist mode.

"Good, as in better than I've ever felt, itchy. Real itchy actually, like I want to go back to the track after everyone leaves and run another batch of 200s just to see how fast I can run them."

"Definitely *do not* do that," Coach shot back, taking me seriously but knowing I wasn't.

"I'm not going to, I'm just sayin'."

"And I'm just sayin' that would be a bad, bad idea."

"I know, I know, and I'm not going to do it. I'm just sayin'."

Coach shot me a you-better-not look just to make sure I wasn't serious.

"You still have your pull-ups to do when we get back anyway," he said.

"Oh, right." I pretended to be surprised.

We ran alongside the trail that hugged the glassy lake, which was still and reflecting all the colors and shapes of the mountains above us. I surveyed every little muscle in my body, checking to make sure every last screw was tight and every last joint smooth and efficient. I felt like a finely tuned machine, ready to roar down the runway wheels up. Everything was in place.

When we got back Coach and I headed into the gym and I pumped out ten pull-ups, barely making it past nine.

37

PAUSE

THE NIGHT AIR WAS CRISP AND COOL, THAT CLASSIC Colorado fall that I loved so much. I dug my hands into my pockets and pulled the collar from my jacket up over my neck. You could almost smell the seasons shifting, but not too soon. It was always in the nights that the shift was more evident. The air got cooler, but during the day it all felt the same.

I walked faster across the orange-lit pavement then slowed to a more pleasant stroll when I was hidden in the shadows.

I took the road south toward the southern tip of the neighborhood where the houses stopped, dropping off to a vast valley below, best known as Marshall Mesa. From here you could see the lights of Denver shining bright into the night and the darkness that separated Boulder from everything else.

The Boulder Bubble.

I wanted to see life on the other side of the bubble without touching it. I liked coming to this spot because it reminded me that there was more to life that what was in Boulder, and therefore more to life than what was currently eating away at my mind.

An hour earlier I sat and fidgeted at the dinner table with my mother. She had cooked my second-favorite meal: pasta salad, so I could reheat it for lunch and make sure my gas tank was full for Saturday's race.

Somewhere back during my junior year it became a tradition of sorts for her to cook this meal on a Thursday night so I could pack it for lunch the next day and eat it cold. This was one of the few meals that tasted great both ways.

I could sense that she wanted to talk or perhaps wanted to be available to talk if I needed it. But the reality was that I was already diving into myself, into the abyss where everything simplified. And talking about it just seemed to confuse the process. It added steps or angles that I had already thought over a million times and talking them out was mentally exhausting.

With the biggest race of my life about forty hours away, all I wanted to do was simplify *everything*.

The day's load of four miles easy wasn't anywhere near enough to take the edge off. In fact, all it did was rev my engine up—I felt better after the run than before it. I was itchy and jittery throughout the four strides we did afterwards, like my legs were ahead of my body again. Every side felt like I was running on full power.

I needed to walk off some of this anxious energy, and I promised Coach I wouldn't run anymore miles.

"Trust the plan," he repeated to me over and over with his hand on my shoulder when I told him how I felt like I needed another mile or two in my legs.

I could walk—that was allowed. And not far. Just enough to relax my mind. He had agreed to that much, so I headed out after dinner to move more wasted thoughts into the trash bin on the bottom right corner of the desktop in my mind.

One of them I wouldn't be able to curb too much: the blue hair didn't turn out anywhere near the shade I was hoping for. The debacle quickly turned heads, and not in a good way.

It was teal.

Some portions were blue, others were teal, some seafoam. All in all, I looked like a punk rocker.

While everyone else in our seven had solid royal blue shades, mine were teal. I tried to shrug it off, but it just added yet another unintended obstacle to the next few days.

After having made it through the halls half the day with my new look, dodging laughs and pointed fingers and hiding faces, the athletic director knocked on Coach's door.

"It's fine," Coach told me later. "We're not changing a thing."

But it didn't feel that way in the moment.

After seeing my State look, the AD insisted Coach force the team to dye their hair back to normal out of fear that we'd humiliate ourselves Saturday morning.

Where we saw team pride and camaraderie, he saw a PR problem if we bonked—or more particularly, if I did.

Coach pushed back and let the old fart know he was letting us do our thing. "School pride," he said.

Nonetheless, the AD left with a steamy red face.

Coach always had our back.

But now I worried too. Our AD's lack of confidence and worry became mine. And it was the last thing I needed to think about—someone else's perspective of my abilities.

The teal hair wouldn't slow me down. And I had never considered the possibility of bonking—bonking was a choice made somewhere well before the race. It was allowing fear to control the outcome. *No.*

Teal hair. Brown hair. Bleached blonde hair. It didn't matter what I *looked* like, the only thing that mattered is what I did on the course.

That was what I always loved the most about running —your performance said everything.

I told myself this over and over while I walked through the night. Talking to myself in my head. If I was talking this way out loud then the neighbors would clearly consider me nuts. But having conversations in my head was about as covert as strolling through the night when no one could see or hear you.

It was the best way to avoid seeing a psychiatrist once a week.

I slowed my thoughts, sending items to the trash bin one by one. AD worrying about my hair—*scrunch*!

Next.

I thought of my father and wished he could be here. We were supposed to talk on the phone tonight since we were headed down to Colorado Springs to stay the night Friday—this would be the last time we could talk since he was a half a world ahead in time, but he never called.

I was angry and relieved at the same time. On one end I wanted to talk to him. I wanted him to be here. But on the other end I was mad that he was gone, and so I didn't want to talk to him.

I wanted two opposing things at the same time. And I knew as much.

The road turned north and looped back toward the bubble, but I stood silent and still in the night, eyeing the twinkling lights a few dozen miles away.

A gentle breeze rolled up the valley, sending chills down my spine. I could hear the creek at the bottom from up here, rumbling along down the rocks, headed east toward the Kansas plains.

I took three deep breaths and closed my eyes, just listening to the world out there and the one inside my head until it all meshed into a white noise of silence, like a fan at night. I counted my breaths and tried to reach three without thinking of anything else, focusing on the numbers so I could keep my mind here, and when I hit three I added another three, then another three. Until I felt entirely present in the moment. Here standing on the edge of this mental and physical abyss.

But here.

38

FRIDAY

MY STOMACH TWISTED AND TURNED DURING THE two-hour drive south down I-25 to Colorado Springs. To detach from my present state I devoured a bag of jellybeans void of the green ones that Lily had packed for me as a parting gift. Sometime in the past few months she remembered me claiming my distaste for the green ones. I didn't even remember the words coming out of the my mouth, but she did, and she was right. The green ones are no bueno.

I soaked in that sugary treat while my eyes scanned westward at the rolling mountains and south to the inevitable Pikes Peak that loomed over Colorado Springs like the Flatirons did over Boulder.

The overseeing god.

Even from an hour away you could see its white peak, contrasting against the vibrant blue sky, towering above everything around it.

By 3 p.m. we were on the starting line at Penrose,

kicking rocks out from what would be our starting block the next day. Teams wearing various colors, reds, whites, blues, and greens from all classifications lingered around, starting at different times. Everyone with their own agenda, and yet somehow it was all the same.

Preview the course.

Get to know the turns and hills, and how steep and how long. *Familiarize* yourself with it all.

In all honesty, I didn't need this preview. I had already done this a million times in my head. I had been here already. I had already run the preview of the course in my head. I knew the gradual hill after the first 300 meters, the loop that turned us back to the crowd around 1k. The bridge. The river crossing. The hill that turned sharp as it zigzagged its way up and up just after the mile marker. The long stretch after that led us to the quiet part of the course, *my favorite*. Then the long gradual uphill that led us to the peak before screaming down and back around, back to life, where the noise from Penrose would return to us. Back by the two mile marker where crowds would line both sides. Onward to the long straightaway that stretched away temporarily before turning back and hugging the creek, twisting and twirling alongside under the trees in the shadows where I would make my last-ditch effort to really wrap this one up. The pinecone I placed twenty meters beyond the second bridge when the path turned left, the final half mile as a cue. Lights out. Then back out into the sun toward the final creek crossing where spectators would linger on the bridge and up the bank to scream incoherent encouragement. Then up the double hill where the crowds only got bigger, louder. Then Penrose would be visible. The stadium off to the right. Onward into the final 300 where it'd get silent for one last time before taking a hard right into the stadium where everyone would see you, and you them. And the noise would be deafening. The first inside and you'd hear it all erupt. *It'll erupt.* Then it's a sheer 200 meter straight-away over dirt to the finish line.

That finish line stood 3.1 miles away from the starting line here. I didn't need to run this course for my head. This was more to take the edge off a bit, if that was even possible.

I stole glances around the area, searching for Grant Hemingway, curious if he was as nervous as me. Perhaps he had already run the course, or perhaps he didn't need to.

We were like Rocky and Drago. Or in my mind at least.

The next twenty-one minutes went by without much thought. I spent it daydreaming about where I'd be, how I'd be feeling, when, where, and how it'd all play out. I envisioned Grant Hemingway hovering over my shoulder where Blake was as we moved around the course.

After lazily making our way up the double hill we were stopped at the entrance to Penrose where a gate stretched across the course.

"No one is allowed into the stadium," an old man with a raspy voice hollered out before we could hop the fence for one quick glance of what it all looked like from inside. Despite having raced here all throughout high school, it was always a challenge to envision the look inside the stadium, because every time I got to this point I was deep in a late-race haze of fatigue.

But I had seen enough.

Besides, the last 100 wasn't about seeing, it was about feeling. And I knew what I'd have to do to get to this point and *feel* the finish without a shadow.

Later than night we anxiously devoured massive plates of spaghetti and bread and all-you-can-eat salads in waves of silence. We depended mostly on Blake or Todd or Chester to entertain us, but the night before State, even they were too nervous to play the role.

Back in Coach's hotel room we sat around for the final meeting. One last "remember the plan."

I took a spot in the corner of the room, the only place I felt comfortable—where no one could see me festering.

And then Coach began. He handed out sheets with projected finishes and our overall score. Where we'd need to be for X, Y, and Z to happen, and if all went well, we could finish on the podium—top three, despite barely making it out of Regionals. *If* we all ran to our potential.

"John, if you can break into the top fifty," Coach said, writing the tally on a marker board he placed over his TV. "You'll have to run with Demerest from Golden and Christie from Standley Lake. You were just behind those two at the Stampede."

John nodded, his tight curls swaying in the motion.

Coach continued as if he were a CEO in a large boardroom in some high-rise skyscraper in New York City, only this was the Holiday Inn off Garden of the Gods Parkway.

"Todd and Chester can team up and finish somewhere between twenty and thirty, you'll want to keep an eye on the two Conifer boys Eckman and Gordon in green or black, they've got a few different uniforms, but they always run together."

"You're so going down, Chester," Todd mused.

"Oh, please, son," Chester shot back laughing.

"As long as you take each other wherever, I don't care who beats who," Coach chimed in with a nervous smile.

He was totally nervous.

We all were.

"And Blake, between fifteen and twenty, we should be in a good spot. Keep an eye on McClay from Fountain."

"Where do you think Vince will finish? Because wherever that is, put me one place in front of him," Blake stated with a straight face.

"Vince should be in the top ten, so if you can get him, you can crack the top ten," Coach said. "Just don't go too crazy early. Remember, the second half is what'll make the difference tomorrow."

"The second mile," Blake said nodding, still holding his gaze before glancing at me, sharing what we talked about through the room.

"Yes, that's where we want to stay awake," Coach said, tipping his pen toward Blake. "And Baxter, between one and five—"

"One, Coach," I interrupted. And I didn't even know I did. I spoke without even thinking, like my tongue and my legs were in the same place—ahead of me. All mouths in the room went silent as everyone's eyes converged on me sitting tightly in the corner, a nervous wreck, but somewhere not so nervous enough to speak up.

"What was that?" Coach said, slightly amused.

"One. Just a one point for me," I said. Anything less would feel like a failure at this point. I knew my limits, and I knew everyone else's too. And I knew if I straddled mine, I'd take that hard right into Penrose without a shadow, just like I had so many times in my head over the years.

39
STATE

I STARED AT THE BRIGHT RED NUMERALS ON THE clock in the hotel room. They looked eerily similar to the ones on the clock at each race. Those curveless red digits, separated by thin lines of fact or fiction.

The clock, like the Flatirons, the overseeing judge of all. The god we must all appease if we wish to be successful.

I wiggled my toes while intently staring at these red numerals in the way I would in another five hours, waiting for them to click to 6:15 when the alarm would go off. But by 6:05 a.m., I couldn't wait any longer.

Close enough.

With another five hours before race time, I took to the streets for a shakeout run—an approved shakeout run.

The sun hadn't yet risen over the plains to the east, but there was a gentle orange hue that lined the horizon as if hinting at what was to come. Above me the morning sky was shedding its dark blue hues in trade for a lighter shade as the dawn became the day. The air was cool and crisp, and soon it'd be warm but dry.

I ran along the vacant sidewalk behind the hotel where streetlights led the way toward the back of a grocery store. I eyed the cracks in the pavement as I jogged loosely over the giant squares, no longer hiding in shadows.

Not anymore.

My mind scanned over every last fiber of muscle in my body, searching for inefficiencies. There weren't any.

I tried to find nostalgia in the moment but couldn't. I thought backwards in time, scanning the season like I scanned my body, reminiscing about it all, and thinking back to that morning run down the South Boulder Creek trail back in August. Months had seemed like years.

Look at us.

Who would have thought?

I couldn't cling to the moment, because my mind was somewhere ahead of me now, somewhere with my legs and body, already on the starting line waiting for an old man in a bucket hat and a Polo shirt to send us off to battle.

While I kept the pace as lazy as possible, it felt as though I could've slept through this run, because I couldn't feel a thing. I was practically numb to any physical exertion, for now at least.

Within minutes the top of Pikes Peak lit up in an orange glow over the white snow, and the sun stretched lazily down the mountain as it climbed upwards into the sky for its daily trek. Soon all of Colorado Springs was out of the shadows along with me, and this run was over with for this time around.

The next few hours came and went in a haze of anxiety.

I sat in the passenger seat of Coach's Toyota 4Runner while he stared at the road from under his navy blue hat. His hands clung to the wheel as he drove. Blake and John sat behind us in silence as we rolled up to the course, which only intensified the flutter of butterflies swirling anxiously in my stomach.

I tried not to look out the window now, because it was all reds and blues and oranges and packs of runners striding one way or another. Worried parents with hats and bags with Gatorade, and kids with painted faces and bodies.

From the outside this had to look a lot like a circus. But for me, these were my people. And I was theirs.

"All right, we'll have some of the JV guys and parents set up the tent so you guys can leave your bags here." Coach went into instruction mode as we stood beside the long row of cars across the street from Penrose. "Just one easy mile for everyone except Baxter, got it?"

Rather than jog along the course like everyone else we set out along the path that meandered west, away from the noise. We ran along in silence—all too nervous to even crack a joke. We knew what was stake. This was all now lights out time.

I lagged near the back, something I had no intention of doing once the gun shot out. Within seven minutes we were back at the tent, and I went out alone. With everyone gone now I went back into myself, back to the usual scan. And it didn't come back good.

My legs, which felt great on the morning shakeout, were now heavy and full of lead. My arms felt like I just done 100 push-ups. I felt as though I went from my 130 pounds of bone to double that of—fear?

My mind nervously raced. Every bad horror of a possibility stormed as the blue sky turned dark inside me. I felt heavy and negative, and I tried to kick it all with a few quick strides.

I forced myself to shift gears, feeling impervious to injury at this point, but I needed to get the shit out of my legs. I needed to jolt the system awake.

Two strides in—nothing.

In panic mode now, I decided to hammer two more. A slap in the face. Perhaps a gut-punch. Go full Fight Club on my ass just to snap out of it.

By the final twenty meters of the third stride I could feel a release, as if the anxiety like a toxin was finally seeping out, and I could get back to feeling fresh.

The fourth stride felt better than the third, and I jogged back to the tent still a little worried about feeling heavy.

"Let's get going, guys," Coach said, standing over the seven of us. "Fifteen minutes. Time to head to the line."

You could hear the nervous tick in his voice. If he could race for us, he would have. He clearly had the energy for it.

I pulled my spikes that still had some grass stains from the Standley Lake race on the sides, *not so white anymore*, and double-laced them up.

"Thirteen minutes, guys," Coach said, circling around us, clipboard in hand. "Time to go."

Parents stood around the tent, eyeing us. Their children going off to battle. Too fearful to talk, to joke. They could feel the mood, the tension in the air. And we could feel their worry. But now there was nothing anyone could do. It was purely up to us now to execute what we had trained for all season.

We loosely said goodbye to our crew and headed toward the line, Coach herding us all the way, our general leading us into battle.

We passed a slew of curious onlookers, entertained by our bluish hair as we made our way to the starting line one last time.

Coach paused for a moment before we slid through the final gate to check in. This is where we would part ways.

He stopped and put his hand on my shoulder, brown eyes darting around at all the colors and then on to me.

"Remember the plan," he said.

I nodded along, staring out at the vast open space beyond the starting line.

"Get out good that first point-one," he said. "And then start kicking."

The last part stopped me in me tracks. *What did he just say?*

Confused, I looked over at him. He cracked a smile then chuckled.

He always knew what to say and when to say it. At the most intense moment of our relationship, he found a way to ease the tension in the air.

"I got it," I said, nervously laughing.

"You know what to do," he said, patting me on the back. "Good luck."

And with that, I was off.

I tried not to look for anyone on the starting line, even though I wanted to know where Grant Hemingway was. I did my best to avoid eye contact and remained within myself, where I needed to be, where I belonged.

Here. In this moment.

A few strides out in the starting area the world began to slow its turn. Sounds muted, and the scent of freshly cut grass was all I noticed. Alongside the starting area were throngs of people, but they meshed into one color, one sound.

I stood in the starting line beside my teammates as the world waited for the starter to send us all in a spin again.

I eased my breathing and found a few yawns which settled my mind. Each exhale released the anxiety of the morning, the week, and the season. Nothing before mattered, and nothing after would.

I stood tall with a light lean, knowing that I'd still need to get out but not too screaming out of the gates only to die later. This would take patience, and I had waited long enough for this moment.

"Racers take your marks," the starter screamed from 100 meters in front of us. "Set —"

I must've hesitated for a second, because I saw the white smoke from his gun drift in tiny curls into the air before my legs got moving.

Two hundred of Colorado's best stormed the field and what was all quiet turned into a haze of noise with no distinct sound. It was *all* sound.

I popped off my toes but kept a cap on effort and speed. We cleared the starting area onwards to the bottleneck, and ran onto the road six wide. I sat in the middle of the pack a few places behind a nameless runner looking for early glory.

He could have it, for now.

Off and away from the crowds we went. I waited patiently to get through this opening mile, knowing that the goal was just to endure whatever pace, but wait wait wait for when the real racing would be—later.

Nobody wins a race in the opening mile, but plenty have lost it there.

After looping around the warehouse we turned back and could hear the roar of the crowd waiting for us. Teammates and parents lined both sides of the dirt road and alongside the hill while one by one eager runners fell like flies around us. I stole a glance left and right, searching for Grant Hemingway, but I couldn't find him anywhere.

By the 1,000 meter mark I ran solidly in the middle of the lead back with Ryley on one side and Vince on the other. I thought of Blake for a moment and hoped he wasn't a step behind us now, because I knew Vince would fade eventually.

We cruised over the bridge and up a gradual hill before turning east toward the first steep hill of the course, the one that zigzagged back and forth up the side of a mini mountain, the one that would get rid of any pretenders. I knew that nothing would be solved before that hill, but afterwards we'd all know who was in the race.

The opening mile came and went in a mild 4:54. I felt comfortable and well within myself, though the only question I had was: how is everyone else feeling?

Up the steep hill I probed Ryley and Vince to see where they were, inching upwards in a fake surge. The Plan called for a few of these testers to throw out some confusion before really throwing down multiple surges up and over the long gradual hill that topped off on the far side.

This was to test the water.

Halfway up the hill Vince was already fading and we weren't even halfway yet, but Ryley clung to my shoulder and I could feel some unknown force moving around behind me.

Once we hit the long stretch that leveled off I took a quick glance to my right, and there he was. Grant Hemingway took powerful strides, eyes down, tight poker face.

He didn't give anything away.

But that didn't matter.

All that mattered was My Plan. My Race. And currently, I was the one controlling the pace.

By the halfway marker the race was far from over, but it felt like it was already down to three. I had Ryley on one shoulder and Grant Hemingway on the other. I eyed the path in front of us and prepared for my attack on the world.

We hit the bottom of the long gradual uphill and I kept a stride lead over Grant Hemingway and faked a failed surged to test him.

He immediately responded, but Ryley didn't make the move as quickly. I sensed blood in the water.

Nearing the top of the hill where the course hit its peak and halfway I eyed the pinecone on the side of the course that I had set the day before.

Lights out.

I eased my breathing one last time, and prepared for an all-out assault. There would be no waiting anymore after this move. After this, it would be pounding away surge after surge until Grant Hemingway was broken. I had no limit on how many surges it would take, it was *whatever* it took.

In the many scenarios I had played out in my mind over the past few months, I figured it'd go all the way down to the final double hill before I shed him—I was ready to take it there.

Just as we neared the point of no return, I felt him inching upwards on my shoulder, as if he was about to make the first move.

No.

I was determined to draw first blood, and I knew in order to beat him, I'd have to be the first to attack, to put him on the defense.

I leaned into my stride, popping off my toes, and pumped hard like the prizefighter at the air.

Off and away we go!

Grant Hemingway immediately responded, but ceded the pacing duties to me. Down the hill we went with him closely chasing. I eyed the ground in front of me, trying to shed any thoughts of what was behind me.

Leave it there where it belongs.

The effort felt manageable, but could I feel myself moving toward that red line a little faster now.

At the bottom of the hill we turned west, back toward where the crowd was waiting and the two-mile marker to catch one last glimpse before sprinting back up the double hill and into Penrose.

We remained locked in our positions, and as we passed the two-mile marker in 9:55 I threw in another wild surge in an attempt to drain his gas tank a little more.

Same response.

Okay, I could keep doing this all day.

We ran down the long straightaway west toward the mountains. For a moment my mind left the present and remembered that talk with Coach about going to a place beyond the mountains.

Stay here. Stay here. Stay here.

I drifted briefly, and when I returned, I could feel Grant Hemingway breathing down my back.

We ran off to the final quiet spot on the course before looping back and into the trees to run alongside the creek, which reminded me of the South Boulder Creek trail. Winding back and forth along the curves, under the trees and hidden from view.

We ran the turns like mountain bikers, and when the trail turned left a little sharper I pressed on the gas pedal again, trying to gain some space on the curve.

And then something happened.

Grant Hemingway didn't respond.

He was still hovering over my shoulder, but I could feel the tether that attached us this whole time was loosening.

I paused for a moment, not sure if this was actually happening. And right when I should've pressed the pedal to the floor, I didn't.

We cleared the trees and cruised back toward the creek crossing where a slew of half-naked teammates with painted chests waited.

I took giant strides across the creek while Grant Hemingway held off from a stride back and then ran onwards into the double hill.

The final dagger.

This is where races are won and lost.

I pumped hard up the hill, waiting to surge one last time halfway up the hill—where people least expected it, and then I hammered.

After reaching the top it was a clean straightaway to the finish. I felt free for the first time of the race. Free from ambitions, free from expectations, and free from Grant Hemingway.

Coach stood beside the white fence just past the top of the hill, and when I cleared the final hill his eyes went wild.

"You're doing it, Baxter! You're doing it! He's breaking! Go! Go! Go!" he screamed at the top of his lungs in a voice of desperation and hope.

My eyes went wide at the possibility that Grant Hemingway was breaking, and in a moment of curiosity I glanced to my right where he had been sitting all morning, and he wasn't there.

Was this really happening?

I set my eyes forward with 300 meters to go, somewhat in disbelief that I was actually here, and all of those daydreams were unfolding out into reality exactly the way I wished they would.

I would not be denied. Not this late.

I kicked hard and could hear the noise of Penrose rising as I took a right turn into the stadium.

It erupted.

Somewhere behind me Grant Hemingway became Grant, and was staggering to stay on his feet. But I was already in Penrose, alone, with the crowd cheering incoherently.

I eyed the finish and focused on putting one foot in front of the other. Avoiding a disaster at all costs.

Each step brought me closer to making this long-held dream a reality, and I soaked up every last voice. Every last smell. Every last painful step over the soft dirt, and then I heard him.

"GO BAXTER!"

Half the stadium was screaming that by now, but this voice was distinct. It had the genuine raspiness of my father, but no—

I glanced off to the right as the finishing chute triangled me in toward the finish line, and I heard it again.

"GO BAXTER!"

My tired eyes scanned the open space between the finish and the stands, and there he was. My father, hands circling around his mouth as he screamed my name, eyes tearing up, next to my mother, whose eyes were already glazed over in tears. Myra with blue-painted hair, jumping up and down in excitement.

This was actually happening.

I powered into the final strides, holding back tears of *everything*.

Tears of victory. Tears of happiness. Tears of disbelief.

This was actually happening.

I raised my arms in victory, pointing toward the sky while my teal hair flowed behind me. And in that exact moment, a photographer from the Denver Post snapped the shot. The very one that would grace the cover of the sports pages for our athletic director to see in the Sunday morning paper.

I ran through the finish as the clock ticked on, arms

wide to scoop up the line and every emotion that went with crossing it first.

I didn't even look at the clock.

The time didn't matter.

I made my way through the finishing chute, feeling the plastic triangles of colors, still shocked at everything. When I envisioned this moment I was lying on my back in sheer exhaustion, fighting for air. But my legs continued, moving onwards on reserves.

"Yes, Baxter! Yes!" I could hear my father still screaming in the distance, making this all the more real.

Through the tiny slits of my eyelids I could see their figures moving through the crowd, down toward the dirt.

My father and mother and Myra came rushing toward me as I cleared the finishing area. My mother wiped her tears and hugged me tight, sandwiching me in with Myra. They didn't seem mind my sweat that painted their shirts in a darker hue.

"I'm so happy for you, Baxter," she said over and over. And in this moment, it sounded genuine. She was actually happy.

When they stepped back my father stood, tears rolling down his tired face, holding a tight smile.

I still wasn't even sure how he got back in time for State.

He stretched his arms wide and bear-hugged me, lifting me into the air. I inhaled that brute scent that always lingered with his presence.

"I'm proud of you, son," he said. "I'm proud."

40

ORIGINS

THE SUN WAS HOT AND THE AIR WAS HUMID, BY
Colorado standards at least. It was late June and the new
coach had assembled the team for the first unofficial practice of the season.

I didn't know anyone.

I was a sophomore transfer from across the state. I was
just as new as the new coach. All I knew about the team
and the school was what I could find in previous results,
and I knew there was one kid named Troy Stark who had
run 17:32—the school record, and another in the 18s.
Beyond that there wasn't a competitive runner on the
team.

Two upperclassmen in basketball shorts jockeyed for
attention while just under ten of us lingered, waiting for
this new coach.

Across the small assembly of runners I spotted a tall,
tan lanky runner who looked to be a senior. This must be
Troy Stark, I thought.

The fastest guy on the team.

I began sizing him up, wondering how I could beat him. He looked like the classic distance runner. The one glaring question mark was on his face—he wore a neatly trimmed goatee.

His full set of facial hair was every high school kid's dream, and here this guy already had one. And he was the fastest guy on the team. The owner of that time was supposed to be a junior.

Maybe this kid was a junior?

He looked older.

The goatee made me question who he was.

Maybe another new kid?

I heard I was the only new one.

I didn't speak once and made it a point to linger behind everyone so as to not gain any attention.

Being social never was my strength.

When the clock ticked to 7 p.m. on the dot and sun still stretched over us, the tall tan lanky kid picked up a clipboard and began to speak.

Pretty ambitious, I figured, for the junior to play team leader just because he was the fastest guy on the team.

The upperclassmen slowly brought down the banter, confused and curious just like I was.

"Uh, well, hello everyone," the tall tan lanky runner said awkwardly.

Was I supposed to introduce myself as the new kid too? I wondered.

And then he continued.

"I'm Coach Andrews, the new head cross country coach," he said.

The nine of us stood silently, wondering if this was a

prank a new kid was playing on us. Now I knew he couldn't be Troy Stark, because even the upperclassmen seemed confused.

"So," he let the let word linger in the air a moment before continuing. "I'd like to get to know everyone, so if you can go around the circle and introduce yourselves that would really help me out."

After going around the circle with introductions, Coach escorted us out and onto the road where he ran alongside us for four miles, talking and getting to know the team he had just inherited.

A gang of misfits.

Really.

The team that year—two years before—were leftovers from wrestling or soccer. Kids who didn't make the cut anywhere else, and so were previously run by the wrestling coach who had his future athletes run to get into shape. The team had zero running ambition, and no State qualifiers.

State wasn't even talked about. It wasn't even a dream.

That first year members of the team I won't name broke over a dozen beer bottles on the dirt roads, a window during wall-ball, and a freshman's collarbone.

And Coach took the squad to State for the first time in over a decade. We finished twelfth then.

Troy Stark led the team with a fifteenth place finish and had run 16:08. I finished fifty-fourth and ran 16:59.

While Coach didn't know he had inherited a squad of hood rats that failed at every other sport, he also didn't know that he planted a seed that year, and the shift in the tides that would come.

Because two years later as a twenty-five-year-old coach

still sporting his neatly trimmed goatee, he trained his first State champion, and led the once squad of degenerates to a podium finish at the State championship.

It's like he always said: Believe in the Plan.

We had barely made it out of the Regional meet alive, but we persevered. We took one of the most unconventional routes to the State meet, but in a way, it made sense, given the history of the team and the journey we had all taken to get here.

I mean, come on, Todd still wore Russell basketball shorts for workouts.

While standing on top of the podium as an individual with my family looking up at me for once was a dream, I got to march back up with our squad, who took third— and missed second by one point to Dakota Ridge.

We didn't mind much.

Third at the State championships after finishing fourth at Regionals was beyond us.

Add that Blake caught Vince in the final stretch—he out-leaned him at the line to finish tenth.

Despite his incredible finish, all he could do after finishing was follow me around as we made our way through the crowd back to our team tent, pointing number one with his finger.

"He's the State champ!" He called out to anyone who'd listen. "Number one! He got *his* crouton!"

Todd and Chester went stride for stride, finishing twentieth and twenty-first, with Chester taking the W over a bemused Todd who was pissed to be so close to beating him, but not.

John had the race of his life and finished thirty-eighth, which sealed our podium finish.

Look at us.
Who would've thought?

41

WALKING BY

I EYED THE NIGHT SKY AS I DROVE DOWN THE winding road, soaking in the crisp mountain air. That blast from the open windows filled my car in chaotic swirls, mirroring the feeling of the day.

It still didn't feel real. Not yet, at least.

Given the results of the morning the squad opted out of a Saturday night at Abo's, and one of the JV kids threw a party at his house for the team, pizza and chips provided.

Even Coach stopped by long enough for the JV kids to TP his car, which turned out to be a bit of a bad deal when a light rain coated it all, making it all the more of a mess to clean up. Days earlier he had made a deal with Chester that if we nabbed a podium finish Chester would get to shave whatever place we finished into the back of Coach's head, and Coach proudly held up his part of the deal.

Surrounded by nearly two dozen kids Chester carefully buzzed a "3" into the back of Coach's head on the back porch while curious parents looked on and snapped photos of the shenanigans.

I watched from afar, soaking it all in, every last little corner, unwilling to let it go but really wishing for silence or movement so I could make sense of it all.

Everyone wanted *the story*—the battleground tale of how I ran Grant Hemingway into the ground.

Don't spare a drop of blood. We want every last punch.

It wasn't until hours later that I learned somewhere up that steep hill after the creek crossing that he stopped and walked and stumbled his way into Penrose a few places under 100th.

Even I didn't believe it for a while until I saw the results, which painted an odd picture of a race blown open early. I ran in such a trance that I never noticed how large the gap between me, Grant Hemingway, and Ryley had been on the field, or that Ryley went on to finish second about thirteen seconds back, followed by no one else for another half a minute.

Over and over I told the story about how David slew Goliath, or that's how it felt at least, since we were all referring to Grant Hemingway as Grant Hemingway.

It was only then that my own team turned the tables and started calling me Baxter Reeves. In one race I had gone from familiar to distant.

That's what a perfectly executed race will do to you, I guess.

By the sixth telling of the tale I was already growing weary of it all, as if I was rewriting my own history in real time, and I only kept on storytelling because Lily showed up late and wanted to hear it from my own mouth.

It was a strange feeling, all of it, though. It was all some unintended result of one perfectly executed race. Like all of sudden everything had changed around me, even though I didn't feel like I had changed at all.

While everyone wanted to hear more and more and more, all I wanted to do was retreat, even from Lily who now looked at me with those big brown eyes with more curiosity than ever before, like now I was something *different*.

To me I was the same Baxter as before. The one in pleated khakis, race t-shirt, and Adidas Marathon 10s. The same Baxter that struggled to talk to anyone of the opposite sex.

But to them I was now Baxter Reeves. The gold medal they all begged me to bring to the party now elevated my status as one whose full name becomes their first name.

Thanks to that one race, I was knighted by the running gods forever.

The more I talked the more distant I felt from everyone in the room and everything around me. I needed to get out and breathe some crisp air, something real, something less demanding of me. The race was enough. The goal was *more than* enough. And now all I wanted was just to *exhale*.

Before the clock hit 9 p.m., I was already exhausted from smiling and taking photos and talking, teal hair and all, that I darted out the back door in a classic Irish goodbye.

I needed to move.

I snuck between the shadows of the houses and out to the light of the front yard where I spotted Coach cleaning the mess the JV kids had made on his car, and I couldn't sneak out on him.

"Tired yet?" he asked, eyeing the house while putting wads of wet TP in a trash bag the parents of the house gave him.

"Exhausted." I started making giant wads from little ones to make the whole process go a little faster, moving over the trunk and tossing them in the trash bag.

"This is what comes with the territory," he said with a laugh.

"Remind me of that the next time I have some big goal in mind," I joked.

We circled his car once more to make sure every last bit was cleaned before he took off. The night was silent, save for the commotion inside. We stood beside the driver's side nodding in approval at the cleaning job.

"Well, listen, Baxter," he said in a more serious tone. "I just want you to know that I've never wanted something for anyone more in my life."

I didn't really know how to respond, so I let the moment linger in the air while trying to find my words.

"I—ugh."

"You know, you did great out there today," he continued, "and I'm really proud of you."

A tension swelled behind my eyes and an unfamiliar feeling overcame me. Before I could stop or divert, my eyes glazed over, and then the words filtered in.

"I couldn't have done any of it without you," I said. "And, I ugh—I just want to say thank you for believing in me."

"I'm your coach," he said matter-of-factly with a sly smile. "It's my job."

"Yeah, but you took my bold dreams and made them possible."

"Your bold-*er* dreams," he quipped, opening his car door and sliding inside.

I stood back and waved while he rolled down his window for one final word.

"Hey Baxter" he said. "How does it taste?"

"How does what taste?"

"Your crouton?"

"It tastes, *great*," I laughed.

I watched him drive off into the night and had no intentions of heading back inside. I had done enough talking and smiling and I needed to breathe some fresh mountain hair. I needed to feel the wind slice through my shaggy teal curls under the night sky, and breathe in the earth so as not to forget this moment.

I hopped in my car with no physical destination. I just wanted to *drive*.

I turned up the volume and let Andrew McMahon's intricate piano riff take me away.

"And these nights I get high just from breathing."

Out in the darkness I swayed with the curves of the road while I stole glances at the starry night sky above me, a canvas of the unknown, of uncharted territory. *A place beyond the mountains.*

Just as they appeared their darkest, a single firework shot upwards into the night and exploded in a million tiny diamonds into the sky.

I wondered what we looked like from such great heights. Tiny specks on a vast rolling canvas. Always changing, always shifting.

I felt my body expanding in the seat, inhaling and

exhaling while my eyes shifted from the road to the sky and back again, the lights of Boulder lit in a circular bubble beneath me now.

My mind wasn't ahead of me, somewhere running another race on another day.

There's no tomorrow or the day after, there's just right here, right now.

And I belong in this moment.

ABOUT THE AUTHOR

As a competitive distance runner, Bobby Reyes won the 2002 Georgia High School Association State Cross Country Championship, the 2005 NJCAA Indoor Mile National Championship, and the 2010 USATF Club 10,000 National Championship in a meet record. He's run three marathons, including Boston, and completed one ultra — the Grand Traverse.

As the editor of Colorado *MileSplit*, a premier online network for all things track & field and cross country, Bobby covers high school cross country and track and field across the state of Colorado, as well as national events. An award-winning journalist, Bobby has written for the *Gunnison Country Times*, *Aurora Sentinel*, *Podium-Runner* (formally *Competitor* magazine), ESPN, and *Colorado Runner*. His lives in Arvada, Colorado with his wife, Liz.

BobbyReyesWrites.com.

CPSIA information can be obtained
at www.ICGtesting.com
Printed in the USA
FSHW021129030920
73441FS